ECHO COMPANY

#1

WELCOME TO VIETNAM

ZACK EMERSON

SCHOLASTIC INC.
New York Toronto London Auckland Sydney

ISBN 0-590-44591-X

12 11 10 9 8 7 6 5 4 3 2 1   1 2 3 4 5 6/9

Printed in the U.S.A.   01

First Scholastic printing, June 1991

For the gang at the Sports Depot —
where much of this was written.

WELCOME TO VIETNAM

CHAPTER 1

THEY SAID it would be hot.

They weren't kidding.

Only, he had figured August-afternoon-in-Georgia hot. Waiting-in-line-at-Cyclorama hot. *Vietnam* hot was different. Vietnam hot was blindingly, numbingly, slam-into-a-brick-wall-at-sixty-miles-an-hour hot. Open-the-plane-door-and-nobody-wants-to-go-outside hot.

Not that anyone wanted to go out there, anyway. After loud bravado most of the way across the Pacific, the plane had been pretty quiet from Okinawa on. And *silent* during the descent to Tan Son Nhut. Especially since the descent was pretty much straight downhill. Didn't seem to make much difference that the seat backs were in their full upright position.

A sergeant going back for his second or third tour, or some gung-ho thing like that, said the pilots took planes down quick to try to avoid getting shot out of the sky.

Cheered everyone up, considerably.

And it was hot. So hot that Michael's dress khakis — so practical for those twenty-hour flights — were dripping wet before he was herded into his first formation. Fifty feet away from the plane.

Some beefy lifer-type was yelling orders, and recruits were falling all over each other in an effort to fall in. Michael slouched, anonymously, near the back. The way he figured it, if you couldn't get a medical profile, keeping a *low* profile was the next best thing.

It was hot. And *loud*. Planes, helicopters, artillery. And sergeants. He had yet to spend a second in the Army during which some faceless sergeant wasn't yelling. Not that he ever listened. What were they going to do — send him to Vietnam?

Might be, that attitude hadn't helped him much in Basic. Probably wouldn't help much here, either.

But, now, ask him if he cared.

Everyone was moving, and he looked around. Oh. Terrific. They were going to go line up somewhere else. Fine. Swell. Hurry up and wait. Typical Army bullshit.

So, they lined up. Again. It was only, what, a hundred and ten degrees — why *not* stand around endlessly with the sun directly overhead and no shade anywhere in sight?

The sergeant up front was welcoming them to the *Ree*-public of *Viet*-nam. Oh, yeah. Almost as nice as getting "Greetings!" from Uncle Sam. Of course, he should have responded, *"Bienvenue!"* — he knew guys who had — but, well. Too late now. He should have gone to *college*. But. Well.

Now, he was in this scenic land — which looked exactly like every Army base he'd ever seen — and there was no way out. Unless he found himself in the Death-or-Dismemberment category. But, knowing the Army, they'd make him finish his tour, anyway. Rules. Gotta follow the rules.

So, it wasn't very scenic, and it smelled like — well, it was hard to say. Not like Thanksgiving dinner. Or a visit to the Hershey factory. More like — a sewage treatment plant blew up, and someone tried to put out the fire with motor oil.

Didn't make him feel like raising his hand

and asking directions to the mess hall.

Now, the sergeant was explaining — at the top of his lungs — that they might have some trouble getting "acclimaticized" to the *Ree*-public of Vietnam. That they were no longer in the US of A.

Could be, he was Army intelligence.

"This sucks, man," someone muttered. "The Army sucks."

There seemed to be general, grumbling agreement.

They stood around some more. Every time a plane took off — which was constantly — hot, gritty dust would swirl around them. A lieutenant, who kept pausing to clean his glasses, informed them that Tan Son Nhut was the busiest airport in the world.

"Guess he ain't never been to O'Hare on a Friday night," someone said, and more than a few people laughed. Michael, among them.

The lieutenant, who gave no impression that he was a leader among men, strode over towards them, with perfect B-movie authority. He stopped in front of Michael.

"You say something, troop?" he asked. Real quiet, and authoritative-like.

"No, sir," Michael said. Real contrite-like.

The lieutenant seemed unconvinced.

This was unsurprising.

"You think it's funny?" he asked.

Also, unsurprising. Contrite-like hadn't gone over well, so Michael decided to try Truth, Justice, and the American Way. If necessary, he would add a firm, manly handshake.

"Yes, sir," he said. "I do."

The lieutenant seemed unprepared. Didn't say much for OCS. He took off his glasses, started to clean them, frowned, and put them back on. "Want to start your tour off at LBJ?" he asked.

Long Binh Jail. "I don't know, sir," Michael said. "They got air-conditioning?"

Around him, grins escaped. Escaped, and were recaptured, almost instantly.

"Give me twenty," the lieutenant said, Gary Cooper-grim, "and then keep it buttoned."

Michael looked down at his fly. "It's not buttoned, sir?"

"Make it a hundred," the lieutenant said, and went back up to the front of the group.

Since induction, Michael had done more than his share of push-ups. He had gotten very good at push-ups. Troublemaking eyes. His grandmother had always said that he had trouble-making eyes. She also said that if you could peel an apple in one long piece, then throw the piece over your shoulder, it would land and form the initials of the person you were going to marry. Michael's little sister Carrie believed this; he did not. However, in recent weeks, what with constant KP, he had had plenty of opportunities to test it — with potato peels — and had seen plenty of initials. "Z" came up a lot. Or "N," depending on how you looked at it.

While he was still doing his push-ups, they all moved again. He was only on seventy-five, but clearly, it was time to eighty-six, so he followed them. He didn't exactly hustle, and heard a "Move along, troop!" from somewhere behind him. He picked up the pace a little — joining the group just in time to stand around some more.

A sergeant — *another* — was calling out names, and the group began to break up, soldiers filing off to various planes, helicopters, and trucks for the next happy stop on their tours. Michael knew that his name would be one of the last ones called — seemed to be that kind of day — and he was right. His particular group was loaded onto buses, with heavy metal grating covering the windows. It felt like a Field Trip for the Chain Gang.

After calling their names again to make sure

the right people were on the right bus, the sergeant remarked that the grating was there to protect them from grenades that passing Vietnamese might throw.

Maybe gratitude wasn't being taught in the old hearts and minds campaign.

"Where you think we're going now?" the guy sitting next to him asked.

Michael shrugged.

"Bet it isn't going to be an improvement," the guy said.

Michael nodded. Safe bet.

Riding to wherever the hell it was that they were going, things began to look foreign. There were a lot of Americans on the road — in jeeps and trucks and the occasional tank — but there were even more Vietnamese. Mostly women and children, with some old men. There were a few small groups of young men, probably ARVN — the Army of the Republic of Vietnam. The ones who were supposed to be on America's side. Still, there was something unnerving about seeing anyone Vietnamese holding a weapon.

Not that he was nervous. Hell, no. He was — hot, that's all. Hot, and maybe a little jet-lagged, and — no problem. No problem at all.

There was something scary about — the hats.

He'd seen pictures of the hats — that famous conical shape — and they'd always seemed sort of . . . quaint. Exotic. Almost festive. But, they weren't. They shadowed faces, and hid eyes, and — not that he was scared. Not that he wished to *hell* he had a damned weapon in case one of these strange, small — they were *really* small — people decided to — well. Not much he could do about it.

Some of the people, mostly children, ran along the sides of the buses and trucks, shouting things. "You buy, GI!" seemed to be the general idea. High, piercing voices that — not that he was scared — made you want to cringe. Made you want to go home. Kids were supposed to shout things like, "You're it!" and "No, *you're* it!", while mothers shouted things like, "Mikey, Dennis, dinnertime!" Normal things. Civilized things. And, hey — what the hell — happy things. These kids didn't look like dinner, and happiness, were regular events in their lives.

"Thought *we* was poor," someone behind him said.

And they were so goddamn small. Even the buildings seemed small, and rickety. Primitive. Apparently, there was no such thing as indoor plumbing, because he could see people stopping — like it was a normal thing to do — right by the side of the road, right in the middle of everything, to go to the bathroom. Jesus. On the drunkest night of his life, he'd still known enough to go behind a tree or something. Anyway, it kind of explained why this stupid country smelled so awful.

"I heard you can't buy Cokes from them because they put ground glass in it," the guy next to him said.

Michael nodded. "Heard that, too." He was guessing they didn't wash their hands much, either.

They rode past fields — rice paddies? — that were a strange, pale green, and actually kind of pretty. There were even a few water buffalo. Unless they were real big, real ugly, six-hundred-pound dogs.

He liked dogs. He liked dogs a lot. His dog, in particular. He missed his dog. Just a little brown shepherd mix, but a hell of a dog. Otis. His sister had wanted to name him Ringo. Yeah, *right*. Most of the dogs in Vietnam, so they said, carried rabies, and if you were stupid enough to pat one, you would probably die.

Don't touch the dogs, don't drink the water, don't trust the children. Nice country.

"Where you from?" the guy next to him asked.

It was the New Guy question to ask. His stomach hurt. He didn't feel like answering. He didn't feel like talking. He didn't feel like making friends.

"Colorado," he said, looking out the window.

"Oh, yeah?" the guy said. "Where?"

Michael looked over. Briefly. "You been there?"

"No," the guy said.

"Denver," Michael said. Close enough.

"I'm from Tennessee," the guy said. "Real small town, real nice."

Michael nodded. Sometimes, it seemed like he was the only guy in the whole stupid Army who didn't have a Southern accent. Apparently, Uncle Sam sent a lot of his invitations below the Mason-Dixon line. Not that he knew exactly where the Mason-Dixon line was — but he had the general concept.

They were going over a river now, across a heavily fortified bridge. The Dong-something River. As usual, when it came to sergeants, he hadn't really been listening. He *had* managed to catch the fact that they'd been riding on Route 316. Which sounded awfully civilized and American for an outdoor latrine surrounded by palm trees and rice paddies and masses of expressionless, tiny, black-haired people.

They were on another base now, Long Binh. An endless expanse of concrete, Quonset huts, Army vehicles, and soldiers. And, although it seemed *too* aggressively American, he could have sworn that he saw a few athletic fields. It was also kind of funny — when in doubt, Americans threw balls around.

When the bus finally stopped, they were told to unload. Double-time, of course. They were at the 90th Replacement Battalion, where they were supposed to wait for their orders to come through for their individual unit assignments. No one seemed to know how long this was going to take, but knowing the Army, it would be days, not minutes.

And yeah, it was still very, very hot.

"What happens now?" a chunky, nervous-looking guy asked him.

Like he had any idea? Michael shrugged.

"What's your MOS?"

Military Occupational Specialty. "Eleven-

Bravo," Michael said. Infantry. Was every guy in the entire Army going to try to start a conversation with him?

"Oh," the chunky guy said, and looked a little guilty.

Sounded like rear echelon. Support troops. "What about you?" Michael asked. Sort of to be polite, sort of to inflict more guilt.

"Well — I'm supposed to be a clerk," the guy said.

Think of the stories he'd have to tell his grandchildren. Not that Michael wouldn't trade places with him in a second, the lucky son-of-a-bitch.

"Fall in!" a sergeant was yelling. "Fall in, dammit!"

They did.

CHAPTER 2

AFTER ENJOYING the sunshine and triple-digit temperature for a while, a corporal squinting at a clipboard gave them their barracks assignments. Low structures, with wooden walls about four feet high, each building surrounded by sandbags. Did that mean they were *expecting* bombs, or was it more like, better safe than sorry? Not that he was about to ask. Wasn't a whole lot he could do about it, either way. There were screens above the wood, going up to tin roofs. Corrugated metal, guaranteed to make any rainstorm much louder than necessary.

There were a lot of sandbagged bunkers and guard towers around, but, as war zones went, things looked pretty routine. A Post Exchange, an Enlisted Men's Club, an Officer's Club, an old metal basketball hoop where some guys were playing pretty energetically, considering the heat.

Inside his particular barracks — hootch, you called it, if you were cool — there were two rows of cots. They were told to select one each — was the Army afraid some of them might take *more* than one? — drop their duffels, and reassemble outside, ASAP. Michael chose one in the back. The canvas was filthy, and looked very uncomfortable, but he would have given just about anything to lie down on it, and sleep for the next ten or twenty hours. No such luck.

They spent what was left of the day waiting in lines. Exchanging their money for MPCs — Military Payment Certificates — Monopoly money, in other words; filling out forms with cheerful information like next of kin, and insurance beneficiaries; going to supply to be issued their jungle fatigues, canvas boots — quick-drying, so they said — socks, underwear, a cap — all of which were OD. OD, being the Army's favorite fashion choice — olive drab. Flattered any face, any figure.

Then, they got to wait in another long line for tepid showers, the water — somewhere between a gush and a sprinkle — draining out of huge oil drums up above. After that, conspicuous in new, perfectly creased fatigues, they waited in line at the mess hall for, also tepid, B-rations. Powdered, reconstituted, not very delicious. Meat — beef, perhaps, gelatinous gravy, watery mashed potatoes — what a treat. But, better than C-rations, which came in cans, and were eaten out in the field. The bush. Out in The War.

His stomach hurt. Not so much that he didn't manage to pound down a few beers at the EM Club, where a Filipino band sang "Ruby Tuesday" and "All You Need Is Love." Badly. Either his alcohol tolerance had gone downhill because he was so damned tired, or this arrhythmic band really *was* just about the funniest thing he had ever seen. With luck, maybe they would sing "Respect," and spell it wrong.

"Jennings, you sorry bum, you," someone said, coming over to slouch against the wall next to him.

Pervis, from AIT. Which was Advanced Individual Training — in his case, Infantry — back in the States. Where the lucky guys who were going to Vietnam got to go after Basic. To learn even *more* about killing. Pervis was a football player from Texas. He'd hurt his knee just badly enough so he couldn't get a college scholarship, but not badly enough to get him out of the draft. Naturally.

"Pervis, you pathetic piece of scum," Michael

said, and they grinned at each other.

"Good to see you, man," Pervis said. "When you get in?"

"Today." Michael slugged down about half of his beer. It wasn't very good — but it was cheap. " 'Bout 1100."

Pervis nodded, and motioned to one of the very busy bartenders for two more. "Where you going?" he asked. "You have any idea?"

"Going nowhere fast," Michael said, and finished his beer.

"I hear you, man," Pervis said, drained his own, then handed Michael one of the two fresh ones. "Come on, you gotta meet these guys."

Pervis was big and friendly — stiff, blond hair, huge shoulders, no neck to speak of — and he already seemed to have a pack of friends. Although Michael wasn't much for gang conversations, he stood around with them for the rest of the night, listening mostly, drinking his fair share. Some of Pervis' new friends were serious rednecks, and there was almost a fight at one point, but before things really got going, the band started playing "Tears on My Pillow" so ineptly that it was hard to do anything *other* than laugh. Maybe bad music was a technique the MPs ought to try.

So, no fight. In a way, he was sorry. He wasn't one to start fights, but he was generally pretty happy to hit back. Only, judging from the way everyone was split up in the place, this particular fight probably would've become a black/white thing — and he hated that stuff. Happened pretty damned often, too, in the Army. He'd kind of hoped that they'd be too busy with, you know, War, to bother with race garbage once he actually got over here, but — didn't look that way. Hell with it, though. Wasn't *his* problem — he'd just as soon keep to himself. Put in his 365, and get on a plane the hell out of here. Get back on his skis, where he belonged. Stay on them forever, if possible.

Canada had some damned good skiing. So he'd heard. Would've been a real gutless move, though. Then again, working on a ski lift, waiting for the draft to come and get him wasn't much better. Hell with it. A lot of guys, it ruled their lives — when it was going to happen, how they were going to get out of it. Trying to gain so much weight they'd be too fat to get in, or lose so much they wouldn't qualify, either. Raise their blood pressure, try to develop a heart murmur. A kid he went to high school with, graduated a year ahead of him, he'd heard gave the sergeant at the induction center a big, sloppy kiss. Got a deferment out of it. "So, what's the story," Michael'd asked him later, "you that bad a kisser?"

The band sang "Louie, Louie."

"Check it out, man." Pervis nudged him. Extremely hard, since he was too drunk to remember how much bigger he was. "They don't know the words, either."

Michael laughed, and drank some beer. "A-yoey-ya-yang, oh, oh" was the lead singer's indistinct and uncertain interpretation. Pretty goddamn hilarious. "Me-ga-ga-go." The more verses they sang, the funnier it got, and Michael borrowed a lighter from one of the rednecks, holding it up in the air. A lot of other Zippos flicked out of hip pockets, and a couple of guys shouted, "Encore!" The band seemed pleased by this tribute, but somewhat confused.

Michael gave the lighter back to the redneck, who said, "Rock and roll, man."

"Here to stay," Michael said, and bought another beer.

The club shut down at 2200, and even though the piss tubes outside — an Army innovation; why not save time and space and just stick a pipe in the ground? — were overflowing, there was a long line. The Army. Always exotic, always efficient. Time to find the side of a building, maybe.

"Don't think I like it much here, Jennings," Pervis said.

"Don't think I do, either," Michael said, and they waited their turn.

It was hard to sleep. For one thing, he was drunk, and his bunk seemed to be spinning around some. For another, mortars thumped and rumbled constantly, somewhere across the base. Outgoing, he hoped. If not, and they had to stumble drunkenly out to some bunker, he was going to regret choosing a cot in the back.

For a third thing, he felt — well, yeah — homesick. He didn't know what time it was, or even what day it was, back in the World, but — well. He felt about ten years younger than almost nineteen. And, the thing was, you got sent to Vietnam, you had to figure on there being a good chance you weren't going home again.

Eleven-Bravo. Shit.

In the Army, you were never alone, and you were always lonely. He was, anyway. Especially here, in this hot, crowded hootch, surrounded by strangers, twelve thousand miles away from — truth was, his stomach hurt, and he was very drunk, and he felt like crying. Not that crying was something he knew a whole lot about — he couldn't even *remember* the last time he — yeah, he could. Not that he ever thought about — oh, hell, he thought about her a lot. Stupid to feel things for someone who didn't feel them back. It was stupid then; it was stupid now. He should grow up, already.

At least, he hadn't cried in front of her. Only later, after he'd dropped her off. He sat there, alone, in his father's old Studebaker for a long time. Got yelled at for bringing the car home late. He didn't argue. Didn't say anything at all. Just went up to bed, and lay very flat, staring at the ceiling, his throat so tight he could barely swallow, no matter how many times he tried.

Kind of like now. Kind of just like that.

Shit. Grow up.

He swallowed a couple more times, took a few deep breaths. *This* was going to be something to tell his grandchildren, all right — "Yes, kids, spent my first night in Vietnam trying like hell not to cry, 'cause, you know, it's not a real tough soldier thing to do." Especially in a room full of total strangers, who would probably make his life miserable if they knew. A couple of times, during Basic, he had seen the pack mentality come out. The hey-I-know, let's-pick-on-the-fat-guy kind of thing. He'd never joined in, but he'd never really stopped it, either. Maybe he would have if it'd gotten out of hand. Maybe not. Be nice to think so.

Actually, among the various snores and restless movements, he could hear a person, here and there, breathing funny. Like they had a real bad cold funny. Maybe he wasn't the only one. After all, it *was* a roomful of kids. Hell, he wasn't sure if he'd met *anyone*, other than officers, who was over twenty. And, except for a few gung-ho wackos, no one wanted to be here. On top of which, hearing actual war artillery, distant or not, was pretty damned scary.

Yeah, he could definitely hear someone crying, very quietly. In a way, it made him feel better; in a way, it made him feel much worse. The poor guy probably thought everyone else was asleep.

Not wanting to listen, or think, anymore, Michael turned over on his side, covered his head with his arm, and tightly closed his eyes. He could still hear it. He pressed his arm over his ear, and did his best to go to sleep.

Happy thought. It was going to be 0500 before he knew it.

*   *   *

He spent most of the next couple of days filling sandbags with dry, dusty dirt. Every so often, they would be summoned to stand in formation, and wait for their names to be called. So far, there had been a John Jennings and a Harry Jensen. After getting his orders, the other Jennings guy grinned from ear to ear, and shouted, "I got motor pool!" to one of his friends, who gave him a thumbs-up back. Lucky son-of-a-bitch.

He ate most of his meals with Pervis and the redneck who hadn't gotten his orders yet, either. Willie something.

As Pervis finished what was left on everyone's trays — including a perfect stranger sitting to their right — Willie read aloud — not very well — from a card they had each been handed during the last formation.

It was rules of conduct, from MACV — Military Assistance Command, Vietnam. The head honchos. There were nine rules, and they were supposed to, what, keep the card handy at all times? Refer to it at key moments? Yeah, right.

The first one was a beauty: "Remember, we are guests here: We make no demands and seek no special treatment." Guests. Made it sound like a real friendly party. A fun time.

"We ain't guests," Willie said. "What's that mean, *guests*?"

"Means you're supposed to bring a hostess gift," Michael said, and drank some reconstituted milk. Yum.

"I don't get it," Willie said, and looked at Pervis. "This guy, he weird?"

Pervis nodded, chewing doggedly. The hamburgers were tough.

"Don't say much, and when he does, he says something weird," Willie said.

Pervis swallowed, then immediately took another bite. "Cold bastard," he said, chewing, very cheerful, "but he drinks good, for a little guy." He belched, noisily, then patted his stomach.

"Here you go." Michael pointed to Rule Seven. "This one's for you."

Rule Seven said: "Don't attract attention by loud, rude or unusual behavior." Pervis looked at the card, then belched again. Loudly and rudely. It wasn't, however, very unusual.

The rules were mainly about how to act around the Vietnamese people — to treat the women with politeness and respect, to make personal friends among the soldiers and common

people, to always give the Vietnamese the right
of way. When you thought about it, it was a
little vague. Were they supposed to give the Viet
Cong and the NVA the right of way, too? Or
just the South Vietnamese people? And since the
North Vietnamese people seemed to look exactly
like the South Vietnamese people, how did you
tell? Did you stop in the middle of a battle to
ask — or would that be loud, rude and unusual?
Just a guess on his part, but that probably
wouldn't be *usual*. Just a guess.

Better keep his mouth shut. Willie would think
this was a weird train of thought. Willie would
have a point.

He looked up at Pervis. "Cold bastard?"

"Well — " Pervis frowned " — you got the
rest of us talkin', and playin' cards, and you just
lyin' there, looking at the ceiling. Didn't mean
an insult, Mikey. Just meant, you ain't much for
talkin'."

Okay. Michael nodded. They had been given
ice cream, and his was almost melted, but he ate
it anyway. Might be a long time before he got
to have it again. He didn't particularly want his
MACV card, and he dropped it on his tray. Definitely a cardinal sin, and possibly a mortal one.

He'd have to find a Catholic somewhere, and ask.

"We're s'posed to keep it," Willie said.

What were they going to do, send him to Vietnam? "I got three rules of my own," Michael said. "Don't need extras."

Pervis belched. "I've heard these rules."

Michael nodded. They were his Army Rules to Live By, and during AIT, he had told them to Pervis on at least twenty occasions. Possibly more. "Keep my head down, keep my butt down," he said, "and — "

"And never, *ever* volunteer," Pervis finished.

"That's right," Michael said, and they both grinned.

Willie looked from one to the other. "Okay," he said finally. "That's not too weird. Let's go grab some brews."

"Sounds good." Pervis stood up with one final belch. "You coming, Jennings?"

Michael nodded, and followed along. Why not.

The next morning, on his way back from breakfast, he ran into Pervis, who had his duffel bag and was obviously on his way out.

"Finally get 'em?" Michael asked.

Pervis nodded. "1st Infantry. Someplace called Lai Khe. Think it's pretty near here."

Michael nodded, too, although he had no idea. There didn't seem to be much to say, so they just stood there.

"Keep that head down," Pervis said finally.

"You, too," Michael said.

They both nodded, then exchanged a brief handshake. There was a truck convoy waiting nearby, the backs of the deuce-and-a-halfs filling with soldiers, most of them new guys. Nervous guys.

Not that they were the best of friends, but — it was awkward. It felt very — real. Very final.

"Well." Pervis picked up his duffel. "See ya sometime."

"Yeah," Michael said.

They both knew they probably wouldn't.

CHAPTER 3

THAT AFTERNOON, his orders came through, too. Echo Company, 4th Battalion, 31st Infantry, in the 196th Light Infantry Brigade, which was in the 23rd (Americal) Infantry Division, based at Chu Lai. All of which meant very little to him. Chu Lai was in I Corps — known as "Eye" Corps — the northernmost military region of the four regions in South Vietnam. The one closest to the DMZ. The one closest to the enemy.

The DMZ was the Demilitarized Zone, a narrow strip of land that divided North Vietnam from South Vietnam. Michael wasn't exactly an expert on the war — other than knowing he didn't want to be in it — but, the basic situation was that it was a civil war. South Vietnam wanted to be independent, and democratic — so they said — and North Vietnam wanted to take over the whole country, and make it communist.

The DMZ was a sort of no-man's-land separating the two halves of the country. The Geneva Convention had something to do with all of this, but Michael wasn't sure what.

He was even more vague on why the United States was here at all, but apparently — so they said — communism was a fate worse than death, and if South Vietnam fell, the rest of the world might follow. Like, one country at a time. America was going to save the world. So they said.

To him, it was sort of like when you were five years old, and asked your parents why the sky was blue, and they said, "Because." Same basic logic seemed to be at work here. On the other hand, what the hell did he know about it. They told him to come; he came. His grandfather fought in WWI, his father fought in WWII, he had cousins who were in Korea. No one in his family ever won medals, or got promoted much, but they always went. And if he asked his father why, his father would say, "Because."

He was supposed to be on a C-130 cargo plane to Chu Lai at 1400. He wasn't quite sure what to do with himself — he was packed and ready to go before 1200 — but, he figured he'd regret it if he went to have a drink. For all he knew, he was going straight into battle. So, he just carried his duffel bag over near where the people going to Chu Lai were supposed to assemble, and sat down on it to wait.

It was very hot. Of course.

Two guys in battered fatigues, with longish hair and nonregulation mustaches, came swaggering by. Combat veterans. And, from the grins, guys on their way home. By looking at the condition of people's uniforms, you could tell how long a guy had been in Vietnam, and how much action he had seen. All of the guys who were on their way home were cocky, but the ones who had actually been in combat — a smaller percentage than he would have guessed — were the cockiest of all. Someone had told him that only one out of every six or eight guys ever went out to the field. Ever. The rest all lucked out with jobs in the rear. With those kinds of odds, he would've figured he'd be safe. Didn't look that way, though. Goddamned Eleven-Bravo. Anyway, these two guys probably weren't much older than he was — but, they sure as hell looked it. Older and tougher and braver.

"Check out the newby," one of the guys said to the other, and they both laughed.

"Looks like he wants his momma," the second guy said, and they laughed again, then came swaggering over.

"Where you going, kid?" the first guy asked.

Kid. "Where *you* going?" Michael asked.

Both of the guys grinned widely.

"Home," the first one said. "Soon's they get me on my beautiful bird."

"Don't worry, kid," the other guy said. "We'll look up your girlfriend, first thing. Keep her company."

Michael shrugged. Truth was, he was a little intimidated by guys who had been out there, and made it back. Especially since he had, what, 362 and a wake-up left before he got to *his* beautiful Freedom bird. But he did his best to look bored beyond belief. To look cool.

"Where they sending you?" the first guy asked.

Michael shrugged. "Americal. The 4/31."

"Buncha losers," the second guy said, and laughed. "You'll fit right in, newby."

Michael shrugged.

"You'll never make it, kid," the guy said. "Hope you kissed your momma good-bye." He laughed again, then went swaggering away. "Come on, Hammer — we wastin' our time with this poor cherry."

"Yeah," the first guy said, then looked at Michael, his expression suddenly much more serious. "Lot of booby traps up there, kid. Keep your eyes open."

Michael nodded.

"You'll be okay," the guy said. "Just don't try to be a hero."

"Count on it," Michael said.

The guy laughed, then went to catch up to his friend.

"Tell my girlfriend I said hi," Michael said after him.

The guy grinned. "Count on it," he said.

The flight wasn't all that long — just over two hours, maybe — but it sure as hell seemed long. There were about twelve of them, packed in among a lot of cargo supplies, and there weren't any seats. So, they had to sit on the metal floor, one strap holding a whole row of them down. It was pretty bumpy and at one point, the guy two guys down from him threw up. Didn't exactly improve the atmosphere.

Chu Lai was hot as hell — naturally — but the base was located right on the South China Sea, so at least there was a — hot — breeze. Except from the air, he had never really seen the ocean, or even been on a beach. A *lake* beach, sure, but that was all. Pretty retarded of him to be excited because he was near a beach, even though he couldn't see it from here.

They were loaded onto trucks, and then assigned to barracks. He and one other guy, a black guy named Calhoun, were the only ones assigned to Echo Company, and since Echo was out in the bush somewhere, they had the hootch to themselves. Kind of eerie. And Calhoun didn't seem to be any more interested in conversation than he was. The 196th LIB was nicknamed "The Chargers," and they had a sort of in-country training academy set up on the base, so that new personnel could get, as some sergeant put it, "indoctrionated." "Orientated." After several days of training, they would be sent out to the field, to their respective units. He could hardly wait.

Out of nowhere, just after they got into formation, it began to pour, and he heard someone saying that the monsoon season was starting early. That before you could say "Jackie Robinson," the whole damned base was going to be a sea of mud.

Oh, swell. What a stupid country.

The actual training wasn't too bad, by Army

standards. The instructors were all combat veterans, spending the last couple of months of their tours in safer duty, and they took it very seriously. Most of them, anyway. The teaching style was a uniformly "Listen up, you assholes, this'll keep you from getting your shit blown away" screaming session, but — he'd rather get the information than not.

The first day, they were taken to a supply sergeant to be issued their weapons and supplies. M-16s, sixteen empty magazines and sixteen boxes of cartridges, four frag grenades, two smoke grenades. Four empty canteens, a rucksack with a light metal frame, a claymore mine, an entrenching tool, a poncho and poncho liner, empty ammo cans, mosquito repellent, a towel, some C-rations, a helmet with liner and cover, extra bootlaces, and Christ knows what all else. And, he bought a K-bar knife off some kid supply clerk, who did business on the side. Better safe than sorry. Once he had all his stuff, the first thing he did was write the initials FTA on the side of his helmet in black ink. Which, of course, stood for Fuck The Army. Might as well let everyone know exactly where he stood.

Then, the training. Almost all of it in the pouring rain. A couple of times, they got to sit in some bleacher kind of things by the beach, but he was so busy watching the ocean, it was hard to keep his mind on whatever the instructor was saying. And he knew it was stuff he had to know, so he was just as glad when they jammed into a hot Quonset hut to get out of the rain.

Among other things, they were taught how to pack the — extremely heavy — rucksacks, and how to maintain the M-16s.

"Clean and oil this sucker every chance you get, so's you don't get greased," this particular instructor advised. "Any dirt, the thing'll jam on you, and you will be one sorry, dead son-of-a-bitch."

They were taught rudimentary first aid — battlefield dressings and all; they went over map reading, and how to choose an LZ — landing zone — for a helicopter. They learned hand signals and ambush techniques. Most of this was review from Basic and AIT, but this time, Michael paid attention. Unless, of course, he saw a really, really cool wave. Vietnam was a whole lot prettier than he would have guessed.

They got lectures on the current combat situation in I Corps, and in South Vietnam as a whole. They got lectures about tactics, and operations. Also, Vietnamese culture and history —

no one really paid attention to that, which just might be kind of stupid and arrogant of all of them — and 196th Light Infantry Brigade history. Everyone slept through that one, too. Stateside, that was the sort of thing you would have to memorize, since officers would give you random pop quizzes, with push-ups and such as punishment — but, here, who really gave a damn?

They spent the rest of their time with weapons, and various booby traps. Apparently, more guys were getting blown away by mines than by enemy fire. There was a kind of obstacle course set up, and if you hit a mine, a powder charge would go off and scare the hell out of you. Sometimes an instructor would scream "Ba-boom!" for no apparent reason, which would scare you even more. Damn near all of them hit at least one powder charge. They practiced setting up, and setting out claymore mines — the Army referred to them as antipersonnel devices. Polite way of saying killing machine. They practiced firing the M-16s, which were lighter than he had expected. Stateside, they had mainly worked with M-14s, which were less powerful and significantly bigger. They also got to fire a few rounds from the M-79 grenade launchers, and a few guys got to fire the LAWs — light antitank weapons. These were kind of hard to aim, and he would have liked a chance to practice. He wanted to give the M-60 machine gun a try, too but so did everyone else, and the bigger guys managed to shove their way to the front of the line, and do almost all of the shooting. Since the gun weighed about twenty-five pounds, and big guys were the only ones who would actually be carrying them in the bush, it was probably for the best.

On the fifth day, he and Calhoun, who he still barely knew, were told to get their rucks together, and be ready to get on a resupply helicopter ASAP. Their regular duffel bags, with everything they'd brought from stateside, had to be checked into a base storage facility, either to be picked up by them at the end of their tours, or sent to their next of kin. Whichever came first.

They were going to the field.

CHAPTER 4

THEY HAD TO WAIT by the helicopter landing pad for someone to find the right mailbag for Echo Company. In the meantime, they loaded a bunch of cases of C-rations, and a few crates of fresh ammo onto the chopper. This was followed by some beer and soda, and three green mermite containers of hot food. Some food had already slopped over the top of one, and Michael smelled something vaguely beefy and tomatoey. Vaguely disgusting.

It was overcast, and hot. The pilot was eager to get going before the rain started, and not shy about voicing his opinions concerning this.

Michael's rucksack was so heavy that it was hard to keep his balance, but he managed to get it on, and stood with Calhoun, waiting. It was hard to swallow. Probably the heat. Yeah, right.

"Don't got a whole lot to say, do you," Calhoun said.

His mind was just about a complete blank. Michael shook his head.

"College boy?"

Michael shook his head.

"You only talk to whitey, maybe?"

Michael looked over at him. Even turning his head made him fall a little off balance from the damn near seventy pounds on his back. Almost half his weight, for Christ's sakes. "Not too good at the New Guy conversation," he said, briefly. "Where you from, you scared, all of that."

Calhoun nodded. "Ain't too good at it myself."

They waited. The pilot and copilot were in their seats now, getting ready to start the chopper up.

"They call me Bear," Calhoun said.

Michael looked over. Calhoun was linebacker big, with a round, young-looking face. His ears kind of stuck out, and he was big enough that a grizzly would think twice before starting a fight with him. "Gee," Michael said. "Wonder where they got that."

Calhoun grinned. "You got a name?"

"Mike," Michael said.

"That's real boring."

Michael nodded.

They waited. Now, a guy was running over with a bulging red sack. The mail. Time to go. Oh, Christ.

"You scared?" Bear asked.

Michael nodded. "Fuck, yes."

"Me, too," Bear said.

They both grinned, but didn't really look at each other. The force of the prop wash was tremendous, and it was too noisy to speak anymore. The door-gunner was motioning them over and, trying to keep their heads low, they ran over to get aboard. Bear made it first, then gave Michael a hand up. He landed heavily on the metal flooring, and was still trying to get his balance when the helicopter lifted off with a sickening swoop. He didn't like helicopters much. Not much at all.

It was too noisy for conversation, for which he was grateful. His heart was thumping away, and felt even louder than the beating of the helicopter blades above them. Weird to feel panic-stricken and expressionless at the same time. One thing he noticed though, once they were up in the air, it was suddenly nice and cool. It felt great. And, a lot of the scenery below was incredibly beautiful. There were bomb craters and all, but there were also picturesque little villages and pretty, square rice paddies. There were so many different shades of green that it was hard for his eyes to take all of them in at once. The Rocky Mountains were, he kind of thought, beautiful in the springtime — but not this beautiful.

"Looks like the damn *Sound of Music!*" Bear bellowed into his ear, and Michael had to laugh. It *did* look like the damned *Sound of Music.* Hills and valleys and all. Only, these hills were probably alive with something else. Something that wasn't going to make him feel like singing.

Not that he was really the singing type. His sister Carrie was always singing, like when it was her turn to do the dishes and all, but he and his brother Dennis had always just figured that she was kind of goofy.

He could hear the pilot shouting something over his radio, but he didn't sound alarmed, so Michael decided not to worry about it. Had enough to worry about as it was.

They were going down. Fast. Crashing? No, everyone looked very calm, so it must be intentional. He could see a very small LZ chopped out of the jungle below, and that's where they were headed. As they got closer to the ground, the door-gunner started shoving everything out. Including him. There were a bunch of filthy, tired-looking guys in the clearing, who grabbed the crates of ammo and C-rations, and then, the helicopter was taking off again almost before Michael picked himself up from the ground.

Yeah, he had fallen flat on his face. Hell of a way to enter the war. Good goddamn omen. He spit out a mouthful of mud, then maneuvered his way to his feet. Someone shoved a case of C-rats into his hands, and motioned for him to follow.

The LZ had been at the top of a hill, and they moved down a ways to what was apparently the NDP — Night Defensive Position. There was a small sandbagged bunker in the middle — the Command Post — and soldiers, maybe ten or fifteen meters apart, were digging foxhole trenches in a wide, circular perimeter, surrounding the CP. Although the beer, soda, and hot-food containers were in plain sight, everyone gathered around the corporal who was holding the mailbag, distributing letters and small packages.

Feeling self-conscious, Michael put his C-rations case on top of the others by the CP, and stood off to one side. He looked at Bear, who shrugged, and slouched against a nearby rock.

A skinny, dark-haired lieutenant holding two letters detached himself from the group, looked them over, then looked at the sergeant, who was black, and very handsome, standing behind them.

"Ask for ten, and they send us two," he said.

Already deep in a letter, the sergeant shrugged, barely looking up. "There it is," he said, reading.

The lieutenant nodded, then reached out to shake their hands. "Lieutenant Brady. Welcome to 1st Platoon. Come on, and we'll get you squared away."

They followed him into the CP, where an even skinnier guy was hunched over a radio, exchanging communications with the fire support base. Out of sight, but definitely not out of mind, since the artillery on the FSB was their main, and quickest, protector. Hunh. Despite the ocean, maybe he *had* been paying attention during those lectures.

"This is Manny, my RTO," Lieutenant Brady said, taking out a logbook. Radio-Telephone Operator. Being an RTO was considered good, because you always knew what was going on, but bad because the radio itself was very heavy, and the antenna made one hell of a good target. So they said.

One of these days, he was going to have to find out who "they" were.

Manny nodded at them, but continued calling in their NDP coordinates. The FSB had to know where *not* to fire.

The lieutenant entered their names and serial numbers into his log, then closed it.

"You get any sort of briefing before they sent you out here?" he asked.

They shook their heads.

"Okay." The lieutenant lit a cigarette, then slowly let out some smoke. "You've come in on the tail end here. We're running S and D's" — Search and Destroy — "right now, with our base back at LZ Joanne. Soon as we mop up around here, we're going to be taking over for the 1/101 up in the Que Son Valley, and the 198th is going to be taking over for us. For now, it's just routine patrols to try and secure the area. We'll be humping out here another five, ten days, then relocating to FSB West. Right now, we got 2nd Platoon a couple klicks below us, and 3rd Platoon is to the east. Any questions?"

Plenty. Michael shook his head. Bear just shrugged.

"Okay." Lieutenant Brady rubbed one hand across his eyes. Didn't look like he'd shaved lately, either. "We'll be moving out tomorrow at 0630. Tonight you two'll pull perimeter duty, but your squads won't be going out on night ambush. Do our best to break you in gradually. Listen to your squad leaders — they know their stuff." He motioned for them to follow him outside.

"Um, sir?" Bear said. "Have you, um, had much contact, sir? Lately?"

Lieutenant Brady shook his head. "Snipers, booby traps. Mostly, I'm losing guys to heat exhaustion. You be sure and take your salt tablets, hear? Malaria, too."

They both nodded. After being inside the CP, it seemed very bright outside. A few soldiers — the ones who hadn't gotten mail, Michael was guessing — gathered around.

"Fresh meat," one of them said, and the others laughed.

Lieutenant Brady ignored them. "Okay," he said. "Jennings, you'll be in 1st Squad. Go find Sergeant Hanson, and he'll tell you what to do.

Calhoun, you're in 2nd Squad, and Smitty over there's going to break you in on the .60."

A little murmur of hostility ran through the group of soldiers watching, coming mainly from the black guys. One of them, about Michael's size and bouncy-looking in his boonie hat, scowled.

"How come *he's* gotta carry the pig?" he asked, indicating Bear.

"Yeah," another guy agreed. "How come you never see no white boy humping the pig?"

Lieutenant Brady sighed, both irritated and patient. "I make the decisions around here, okay? You all go dig in now. Get yourself some chow first."

"Still don't see why the white boy gets off easy," the bouncy-looking kid grumbled. "Ever' time we get a brother in here, you just surely *know* that he — "

Lieutenant Brady sighed again. "Just take a look at them, Snoopy." He gestured towards Michael. "This one isn't even going to be able to hump his ruck, forget the .60. Calhoun here's got a good forty, fifty pounds on him. So, enough with the goddamn race shit, okay? Go get some chow." He looked at Michael and Bear. "You, too. Get yourself something to eat, then check in with your squad leaders. 1st Squad's dug in down there, 2nd Squad's over here." He nodded, once, then went back into the CP bunker.

Bear looked at Michael, shrugged, and headed for the food.

Michael, personally, wasn't hungry. Truth was, he hadn't been hungry since he'd set foot in the Ree-public of Vietnam. The truth also was, he wasn't sure if he was ever going to be hungry again. Not for 357 and a wake-up, anyway.

"So, Meat." The little bouncy guy — Snoopy? — stepped up to him, arms folded. "You don't look too tough."

Michael looked right back at him. "Tough enough to kick *your* ass and come back for more."

"Oh, yeah?" Snoopy looked him right in the eye, then grinned unexpectedly. "We'll see. Come meet the guys."

"Yeah, you poor sucker," a guy lounging on the ground with a tin plate of lukewarm American chop suey — it looked like — and a beer said. "The other cherry's lucky, even if he do have to carry the pig. *You* got put in with the kindergarten."

Snoopy did not seem to be offended. "Yeah, well, y'all in Two Squad only *wish* you could get out of nursery school and into our kindergarten." Then, he looked at Michael. "That's Thumper. He's good when the shit starts flyin', but other than that, he is nothing but a fool."

"You the expert," Thumper said, and drank his beer.

"So. Meat," Snoopy went on conversationally. "Seems to me like you are one *deeply* pathetic cherry. You know this about yourself?"

"I've been told," Michael said. "And my name's Mike."

"I like Meat better," Snoopy said, then pointed ahead at two guys slouched in one of the trenches, eating, while one of them read a letter aloud. "Now, the real ugly one's Jankowski, our radio boy, and that there is my man Viper. Seeing as he's a brother, you just *know* they got him carrying the pig, which they surely do. Boys, this is Meat. He is one *very* pathetic cherry, but don't worry — Snoopy, here is on the job." He paused, briefly, then rubbed his stomach. "And hungry as can be, so if y'all promise not to go nowhere, I'll be back in a mad minute." He grabbed a tin cup from a nearby rucksack, and headed for the mermite containers. "Look out, boys! Wild-man coming through!"

Michael watched him go. "Lot of energy."

Jankowski and Viper both nodded. They both looked tired. Tired of Snoopy, or tired of the war? Hard to say.

Viper, who was tall and lean, with cinnamon-colored skin, put a hand out. "Good to have you, Meat. Always need an extra leg around here. Drop your ruck, and stay a while."

Michael felt a little shy, but he let the rucksack fall, and sat on the edge of the trench. Two guys the next trench over were filling sandbags, and singing "The Crystal Ship." Pretty well, actually. Pretty loud, too.

Jankowski saw him looking, and nodded. Even sitting down, he was kind of gawky, and looked like he belonged in a marching band somewhere. "Yup," he said. "They're with us. We've got the loudest damn squad in Vietnam. J.D., Finnegan, come meet the newby!"

The two guys came ambling over. They were both clearly Irish. The smaller one had very black hair, very blue eyes, and a face like a sly leprechaun. "Butter wouldn't melt in his mouth," Michael's grandmother would say. The kind of face you'd expect to see passing the collection plate, but then you'd wonder if the collection was going to make it safely back to the altar or not. The other guy had a lot of red hair and freckles, and the words "Morrison rules" scrawled across his helmet. Michael's grandmother would have taken one look and said, "Corn-fed."

"Finnegan," Jankowski said, indicating the black-haired guy, "and that's J.D." He pointed at the red-haired guy.

"That's Corporal to you, son," J.D. said, and sat down next to Viper, showing him a little handful of letters in pink envelopes. The perfume on the letters was so strong that Michael could smell it from several feet away.

Finnegan looked at Michael critically, then at the others. "What is this, Munchkin-squad? How come we get all the little guys?"

"You aren't exactly King Kong, son," J.D. said, reading — or, probably, rereading — one of the letters with a fairly goofy-looking grin on his face.

"Well, no," Finnegan agreed. "That's why I like having guys like Viper and the Sarge to stand behind." He grinned at Michael, the grin making him look even more like a larcenous leprechaun. "Got a name, Munchkin-man?"

This kid had an inch on him — *maybe*. "Mike," Michael said.

"No way," Snoopy said, coming over with his tin cup full of chop suey, and a couple of cans of beer. "His name's Meat — now and forever." He tossed Michael one of the beers. "Here. Don't ever go saying I didn't do anything for you."

Michael caught the can automatically, and opened it, realizing — too late — that Snoopy had probably shaken it up first so it would spurt all over him. He waited for the foam to die down, then took a sip. "Thanks," he said, deciding that he was too cool to wipe any of the beer off his face.

Snoopy grinned. "Don't mention it," he said.

The sergeant Michael had seen earlier came over with a Coke and a cigarette.

"Good," he said. "Everyone's here. We've got a couple things to go over." He nodded at Michael. "I'm Hanson. Any problems you got, you come to me. What's your name?"

Michael started to say, "Mike," looked at Snoopy, and sighed. "Meat," he said. "They call me Meat."

CHAPTER 5

SERGEANT HANSON sat down, sipping his Coke very slowly, as though it were the king's ambrosia.

"Aren'tcha going to eat, Sarge?" J.D. asked.

Sergeant Hanson shook his head, and sipped his Coke. "Don't think I've been hungry since Dien Bien Phu."

J.D. and Finnegan looked at each other. Frick and Frack, Michael was guessing.

"Wow," Finnegan said. "He would've been, like — seven?"

J.D. shook his head, impressed. "All that time not eating, and look at how nice and big he is today."

Finnegan nodded. "A fine figure of a man."

J.D. nodded, too. "Must've been something in the water." Then, he looked at Michael. "Hey!

53

You bring any Kool-Aid, or tabasco with you?"

What? Michael shook his head.

"Oh." J.D. frowned. "Then, what good are you?"

"You two want to keep your mouths shut for, say, twenty seconds?" Sergeant Hanson asked.

"Yes, sir," J.D. said, and punched Finnegan in the arm.

"Count on us, sir," Finnegan said, and they both looked very serious. Well — sort of.

That guy Thumper might have had a point with the kindergarten thing. Not that these guys weren't kind of funny. Michael looked at Snoopy, who had his mouth open, and appeared to be a millisecond from making a comment. Sergeant Hanson noticed, too, and pointed a warning finger at him. Snoopy instantly subsided.

"Thank you," Sergeant Hanson said. "Now, we're going to hang tight tonight — we've got a lot of humping tomorrow. 3rd Squad's going to pull LP, so I want all of you real alert on the perimeter." He looked at Snoopy. "You dug in yet?"

"Meat here's going to help me," Snoopy said.

"Well, hustle it up. I want everyone settled in

before we lose the light." Sergeant Hanson took one last puff on his cigarette, then stood up. "Viper, Jankowski, you take the middle. Any trouble," he said to the rest of them, "you let Janny know, so he can get a sit-rep back to the CP. Make sure to check your claymores; we don't want a repeat of LZ Nancy."

They all looked grim, leading Michael to believe that someone had set his claymore up backwards in the relatively recent past, with ugly results. Claymores were supposed to explode forward with a charge of six hundred steel balls. Anyone caught in the blast was, as one of the Charger instructors would put it, one sorry, dead son-of-a-bitch. Sometimes, so they said, the Viet Cong would sneak up silently, and turn the claymores around without anyone seeing them do it. With, again, predictably ugly results.

"Noise discipline, okay?" Sergeant Hanson said, looking at Snoopy, J.D., and Finnegan in particular. He looked at Finnegan twice. "I don't want to have to come over here."

"Okay, Dad," Snoopy said. "If you promise I can have the car Friday night."

"How come you get the car?" Finnegan asked. "You always get the car."

" 'Cause he likes me best," Snoopy said. "That's how come."

"I don't think so," J.D. said. "In fact, I think *I* should get the car, and you two little boys should — "

"*I* think that if I hear anything but the sound of digging in the next few minutes, I'm going to know some very unhappy soldiers who are going to pull latrine duty forever," Sergeant Hanson said.

"Think I hear my shovel calling," Finnegan said, and headed for his trench.

"Tell it to shut up," J.D. said, going after him. "It's very loud. We're in a war zone, for Christ's sakes."

Sergeant Hanson looked at Snoopy, who nodded, and headed for the trench on the other side. Then, he looked at Michael, indicating his helmet strap.

"Leave it undone, okay?" he said.

Michael instantly unbuckled it, wondering why. Maybe he'd rather *not* know.

"Good," Sergeant Hanson said. "And thread one of those dog tags onto your boot, okay?"

Michael nodded, uneasily.

" 'Case you gets your head blown off, and they don't know who you are," Viper said lazily.

Jesus. Michael slipped one of the tags off the chain around his neck, and bent to lace it onto his right boot.

"Good. Either tape up the other one, or keep it in your shirt. Don't want it catching any light," Sergeant Hanson said. "And remember, no cigarettes after it's dark. And keep your detonators handy. You switch off with Snoopy every two hours. Keep alert. We're going to get some rain, but that doesn't mean Charlie won't be out in it. Keep your eyes open, and your toilet paper dry. You got questions, Snoopy knows what to do."

"He does," Viper said, as Sergeant Hanson walked away. "He and the Mick brothers might yap a lot, but when it comes down to it, they're right there. Hell, J.D.'s got eight months in-country — he's probably one of the best in the company."

Hunh. Go figure.

Jankowski nodded. "Hang loose, Meat. Tonight's just a walk in the park. Don't go firing for no reason — that'll just give them a fix on your position. If they're out there, the LPs should pick it up first, and L-T or Sarge'll come over to let you know. So, keep it on safety 'less you're *more* than sure."

Michael nodded, hoping he didn't look as uneasy as he felt. Already, there seemed to be too much to remember. His guess was, it was going to be one hell of a long night.

357 and a wake-up. Seemed like it had *already* been a year.

Snoopy had the trench pretty well dug, but Michael took out his brand-new entrenching tool — shovel, to civilians — and helped him finish. The hole was about six feet long, and four or five feet deep, with a double row of sandbags up front — with room to rest machine guns — and along the two sides. The back was open. Snoopy also dumped a couple of sandbags into the foxhole for them to sit on when they weren't on guard.

"Makes an okay pillow," he said.

Michael nodded. It was getting darker, and his throat was getting tighter.

"We got claymores there, there, and there," Snoopy pointed. "You gotta piss or anything, you best do it now."

Michael nodded. Good idea. When he climbed back into the trench, it was almost dark. Snoopy was spreading mosquito repellent all over himself.

"Put the bug juice everywhere, man," he said. "Not that they won't feast on your fresh white meat, anyway."

Michael frowned, but pulled the little bottle of bug juice out of his rucksack. It smelled awful, and he hoped the mosquitoes were going to hate it as much as he did. Christ, there were a lot of them. No wonder they had to take so damned many malaria pills.

"Maybe we should call you White Meat," Snoopy said, thoughtfully. "Think I like that better."

Michael frowned at him, but kept rubbing the repellent into his face and neck.

"Not just the skin, man," Snoopy said. "Get your clothes, too. They're real stubborn little bastards. Do it around your cuffs; helps keep 'em from getting inside." Finished, he stuck the little plastic bottle in the side of his boonie hat. "Maybe we'll call you Breast Meat."

Michael scowled at him, but didn't say anything.

"*Chicken*-Breast." Snoopy nodded. "Yeah, that's a good name for you."

Okay, enough of this already. Michael whipped his K-bar out of the sheath on his hip, and pointed it in Snoopy's direction.

"You call me Chicken-Breast," he said calmly, "and I'll have your throat slit before you get the 'ick' out."

Snoopy grinned. "You're okay, Meat. Think you and I are going to get along just fine."

Michael put the knife away, and went back to the bug juice. A lot easier to be tough around someone your own size. He *wasn't* a Munchkin, but then again, he'd always wanted to weigh over one hundred and fifty. He was never going to be six feet tall, but he had hopes for — five-ten. Fading hopes.

"You gotta realize though, Meat," Snoopy said, lining up the detonators. "I never *do* make a friend who's one of the pale folks. So's you and I'll just be pretend-like friends."

"Right," Michael said, shook his head, and stuck his bug juice under the band running around the outside of his helmet. When in Rome . . . What the hell was that from, anyway? He wasn't stupid, but he wasn't what you'd call a real book guy. Nothing to be proud of, considering if he *was,* he'd be in college, not in this stinking, hot, stupid place, with mosquitoes buzzing all around his head like they were trying to drive him insane. They were doing a good job of it.

It was pitch-dark out now — scary — and when Snoopy spoke, Michael couldn't help jumping.

"Couple rules out here, Meat," Snoopy said, and it was sort of jarring to hear this bouncy guy sound so serious. "You break either, you will *surely* catch hell for it. Don't ever fall asleep on guard, and don't *ever* get high in the bush. We get to the rear, you do whatever makes your little self happy, but out here, that kind of thing'll get your butt fragged. You hear me?"

Michael nodded, forgetting that it was pitch-black, and Snoopy couldn't see him.

"I don't hear *you*," Snoopy said, still very serious.

"Loud and clear," Michael said.

"Good," Snoopy said. " 'Cause it's one they don't tell you twice. You *really* can't stay awake, I'll pick up for you, but — don't do it regular."

"Nope," Michael said.

"You want the first watch?"

No. Not even one small chance in hell. "Okay," Michael said. You were looking for strength of convictions, he was the guy to see.

"Good," Snoopy said. " 'Cause I am one tired son-of-a-bitch."

Michael swallowed, and picked up his M-16,

resting it up on the sandbags. He could hear Snoopy moving around the trench, trying to make himself comfortable in his poncho liner.

"Remember, man," Snoopy said, sounding sleepy. "We got trip flares out there. You're gonna hear noises, but if it's really gooks, they'll prob'ly set 'em off, and you'll *see* 'em, too. Huck a grenade first, don't be giving away our position."

Gooks. Scary to think the Army had *taught* them to call people "gooks."

"Yup," Michael said, trying to sound cool, aware that the only thing his voice sounded was high.

"Everyone's scared, Meat," Snoopy said. "Sarge says, soon's you stop being scared, you're maybe *one* second from gettin' zapped."

Hard to decide if that was comforting or not.

Snoopy yawned. "You got a watch, man?"

Michael swallowed. "Yeah." Still high.

"Wake me up in two," Snoopy said, and then, it was quiet.

It was *very* quiet. Except for mosquitoes, and a couple of bird noises. And, for a minute, he thought he could hear whispering in the trench to his right — 2nd Squad? He hoped? — but then, it stopped.

Was it this dark because they were in the jungle, or just because this place was downright evil? Michael's throat hurt, and he wanted to clear it, but he knew he wasn't supposed to make any noise.

He flinched as he heard the thud and whistle of artillery, somewhere not too far away.

"H and I," Snoopy mumbled, apparently just awake enough to have felt him jump. "Don't mean nothin'."

H & I. Harassment and Interdiction. The idea was, back at the firebase, that based on intelligence reports, and taking into account the location of friendly forces, artillery would send a bunch of rounds out where they *thought* the VC might be. Maybe the rounds hit people; maybe they didn't. But, the Army liked to stay busy.

He squinted, trying to see through the darkness, through the jungle ahead. How could it be so completely dark? It wasn't like he'd never been outside at night before. Of course, the backyard probably didn't count. His family was — suburban. They lived right outside Denver, so they were *near* the mountains, but they weren't the camping and hunting and fishing types. He'd never wanted to be, either. He'd been out late with the ski patrol, naturally, looking for jerks who had skied off-limits, and beyond their limits, but the *point* was to be able to find each other in that situation, so everyone would have lanterns, and flashlights, and all. Plus, when there was snow on the ground, it never really seemed dark.

Sitting here thinking about home was probably a good way to become one sorry, dead son-of-a-bitch.

There was a little bit of wind — it felt moist, and the mosquitoes were enjoying it, *and* him. He could hear branches rustling. Just the wind, or Charlie, smart, and swift, and tricky as hell? Supposedly, they could snake right up to you without making a sound, and you wouldn't see them until the second before you died.

Jesus.

He took out his watch, keeping the dial covered with his hand. They said that VC could see the little luminous glow, if you were too stupid to keep it hidden. He felt stupid. Like he didn't know anything, like each breath was probably going to be his last.

And what if something *did* happen? Hell, he'd probably just hide until it was over. They would all hate him, but, so what? A couple of months getting yelled at by some redneck drill sergeants, and he was suddenly supposed to be transformed into a lean, mean, fearless fighting machine? He didn't even know why he was here, for Christ's sakes. He didn't *want* to be here. He didn't deserve to — what was that?!

He gripped the M-16 tightly, feeling his finger tremble against the safety. A twig snapped. For sure, a twig had snapped. They were out there. Was anyone else awake? Was he the only one who had heard it? Were they coming?

No more sounds. The wind. His heart, trying to pound right out of his chest, and he had a sudden vision of it flopping around in the dirt, while he looked down stupidly at the hole in his chest.

Only — what if that *was* a vision? Extrasensory, and all. Maybe that's where they were going to shoot him, and that's how he was going to die, and — it was very, very quiet. How could a platoon that had been so noisy just a little while ago be so silent now? What if they were all gone? What if they were all dead, killed by sneaky, swift VC? But, Snoopy was here; Michael could hear him breathing. The others — guys he didn't know from this hole in the ground — had to be here, too. Noise discipline, that's all. Just a walk in the park.

He could feel himself perspiring, and he wiped his face against his shoulder, not taking his eyes off the black jungle ahead. He must have wiped off some of the mosquito repellent, because they were immediately at him. On him. All over him. Carefully, he moved his left hand to his helmet, taking out the bug juice, squirting a little more on his face. It stung a little.

No sounds. No light. No nothing.

He slipped his watch out again, covering the dial with a shaking hand.

It had only been twelve minutes. Christ. He had another one hundred and eight to go.

CHAPTER 6

AFTER ABOUT AN HOUR, it began to rain. Lightly, at first; then, more like a downpour. *Exactly* like a downpour. He couldn't see anything, he couldn't hear anything — other than rain — and he wasn't sure what he was supposed to be doing. Then again, if he was going to get — if something terrible was going to happen to him here — maybe he'd rather not see it coming.

But, he was responsible for other people now, not just himself. He didn't know them, but — truth was, he had never been much of a one for teams. More than one coach had pointed this out to him over the years. Baseball was okay because it only *seemed* like a team game, when it wasn't. You hit by yourself, you caught the ball by yourself, you pitched by yourself. In fact, the best way to win was to have seven guys who were loners, and a shortstop and second baseman who were good friends. Yeah, he liked baseball just fine. Played outfield, mostly. Because of the altitude where he lived, the ball really carried, and you could pretend you were a power-hitter, even if you wouldn't be at sea level. He was fast, and he had good hands, so he'd also been on the football team for half of the season his last two years in high school. He could never manage to be quite as gung ho as the coaches wanted, and somewhere during the season, they would all agree that his time might be better spent elsewhere. Hell, he couldn't even manage the *ski* team. Practices, and rules, and buses to catch all the time. Who needed it.

So, here he was in the Army. The Army must be what teams were like in Hell. But, he still felt responsible. If he screwed up this time, they weren't just going to lose some stupid game — someone was going to get hurt. Killed.

Jesus. Was he *really* here in goddamn Southeast Asia?

This wasn't going to work for him. This wasn't going to work at all.

He was getting soaked, but he was afraid to reach down inside his ruck for his poncho. Afraid to take his eyes off the perimeter. God, if only he could *see*.

Hard to believe, but he hadn't heard Snoopy move at all. They were getting drenched, and the kid didn't even wake up. Said a lot about the kind of conditions these guys were living under. About what they found routine.

War. He was in a *war*. Un-goddamn-believable. It didn't seem like a war, it seemed — like a really bad movie you'd watch on Sunday afternoon. Like he was playing a part. Badly. Like he'd wake up, and his father would be yelling for him to get downstairs and mow the lawn. *Now*.

It was pouring, and the mosquitoes were still all over him. And there were people who lived here by *choice*?

He felt a sudden wave of sleepiness, and shook his head, trying to focus. A year. This was going to be his life for the next year. If he was *lucky*. Christ. Kennedy never would have let this happen. Kennedy might have gotten them into it in the first place — his father said it was Eisenhower — but he never would have let it go this far. And, hell, his parents and people had voted against Goldwater because this was precisely what they were afraid would happen. That American boys would be sent overseas to fight some war no one understood, in a place a lot of people wouldn't even be able to find on a map. Including him, up until recently. Yeah, well, love it, or leave it, right? Only, the way it had worked out, it was love it, *and* leave it. If people in the neighborhood ran into his parents, they would say, hey, haven't seen Mikey around lately, and his parents would say, that's because he's in Vietnam. And the people would say, oh, well, he always was a screw-up. He always had been, but — he didn't deserve this. No one did.

It wasn't a movie. It was real. He and Bear got off the chopper, clean and healthy and nervous, and they were immediately surrounded by a lot of grungy-looking guys, whose uniforms were torn, and hanging off because they were so skinny, who looked too tired to function, who were covered with cuts and scratches and what he was afraid was jungle rot. Gross, fungus-y rash. It looked like the skin was just decaying right off some of their bodies. And now, he was part of it. Christ Almighty.

He checked his watch, the face somewhat clouded by moisture. Snoopy's turn. Thank God. He had even given him ten minutes extra sleep.

Still watching the perimeter, he bent enough to touch Snoopy's leg, to shake him awake.

Snoopy was instantly alert, grabbing for his gun, obviously afraid that they were under attack, his breath coming in short bursts.

"It's your turn, man," Michael whispered.

"What? I mean, yeah." Snoopy shook his head, eased the gun down, then climbed stiffly to his feet. "Shit. That you, Meat?"

"Yeah," Michael said. He hadn't even had the name Meat for twelve hours, and he was already answering to it.

Snoopy yawned. "See anything?"

"I don't know," Michael said. "I don't think so."

Snoopy laughed softly. "I hear ya, man. Get some Z's."

Michael nodded, slipped his poncho and poncho liner out of his rucksack, and wrapped them around himself before lying down in the puddle that was now the bottom of their trench.

"I fucking hate this place," Snoopy whispered.

"Me, too," Michael whispered back, and closed his eyes.

He wouldn't have guessed that he would be able to fall asleep, but he did. Almost instantly. The next thing he knew, he felt a hand shaking his boot, and he scrambled up the same way Snoopy had, fumbling for his gun.

"Welcome to the war, man," Snoopy whispered.

Michael nodded, wiping some of the rain out of his eyes, giving his head one hard shake to try and wake up, then staring out at the dark, rainy jungle.

He had been looking straight ahead for about an hour, his eyes and mind numbed by the monotony, when he heard a noise behind him and whirled around, shaking all over, ready to fire the M-16.

"Take it easy, kid," a voice whispered.

Sergeant Hanson. Michael swallowed, and lowered the gun, his hands shaking even more.

"You doing okay?" Sergeant Hanson whispered.

"Yes, sir," Michael whispered back, still shaking. Good thing they were told to keep the damned weapons on safety.

"Save 'sir' for the officers," Sergeant Hanson said, "and for the rear. Keep alert now, okay?" Then, he was gone into the rain, as swiftly as he had appeared.

It took just about the rest of his guard shift for Michael's heart to stop racing. The Army had to be crazy, putting lethal weapons into the hands of scared kids. What the hell was he doing here? He wasn't going to be good at this. He was going to let everyone down.

It stayed quiet. He got wetter and stiffer, and covered with more mosquito bites. The poncho didn't help much. The water in the foxhole was now a couple of inches deep, and he felt as thoroughly miserable and uncomfortable as he could ever remember being.

This time, when he had to wake Snoopy up, he was more careful, and Snoopy's reaction was less violent. They switched places, Michael curling up with his head on one of the sandbags, most of the rest of him under water. Hopefully, if he started to drown, he would wake up.

"See anything?" Snoopy whispered.

"Just the Sarge," Michael said.

"He scare the pants off you?"

Completely. "Yeah."

Snoopy laughed a little, and Michael closed his eyes. Again.

The next time Snoopy woke him up, he was so cramped and exhausted that it was hard to get up. Kind of an understatement. His left leg was asleep, but it would be too noisy to stamp on it in the water, so he just gritted his teeth, and kept his weight on his other foot.

"Wake me up right before six," Snoopy whispered. "So's we have time to eat before we pull out."

"Okay," Michael whispered, and did his best to stare alertly into the rain, and night.

His best sucked.

The rain stopped around five-thirty, and the only sound was an ominous dripping. He felt clammy and disgusting, and wrinkled all over. Especially his feet.

At five of six, Michael touched the tip of Snoopy's boot. The sky was beginning to brighten, and he could distinguish the outlines of trees and bushes and foxholes around him. Snoopy sat up with an effort, in a good three inches of water.

"Shit," he said, looking around.

Michael nodded. Vietnam didn't seem like the kind of place where you felt like saying "Good morning." It was lighter now — dawn apparently came in a big hurry here — and he opened his rucksack to get out some C-rations, and heat tabs. Almost everything was completely soaked.

"Stuff you don't want getting wet, stick in an ammo can," Snoopy said.

Michael nodded. Too late now. He looked around cautiously, then climbed out of the foxhole enough to sit on top of some wet sandbags. He could see other guys in the platoon doing the same thing, all around the perimeter.

"Those tabs're no good," Snoopy said. "Let me light up some C-4."

Plastic explosive.

"It won't — blow up?" Michael asked, feeling stupid.

"Not without a detonator." Snoopy paused. "I don't *think*." He grinned at Michael's expression. "Just bustin' you, man." He took a small, empty, scorched can out of his rucksack, then used his knife to cut a piece of C-4 off a candy-bar-sized chunk, and dropped the quarter-sized piece into the can.

Michael watched all of this, taking mental notes, then looked at the main dish from the C-ration he'd pulled out. Franks and beans. Whatever. He was too hungry to be picky. He took out his P-38 — a small metal can opener — and ran it around the edge of the can to open it, bending the lid back to use as a handle.

"Save the heat for coffee," Snoopy said.

Michael nodded, and took out his tin cup. He poured the little packet of C-rat coffee into it, filled it with water from one of his canteens, then held it over the C-4, after Snoopy lit it with his Zippo, shaking the water off first. Snoopy was right — it burned hard and hot. And fast.

"Fuckin' A," Snoopy said, when he opened his C-ration box. "Sliced beef."

The water was already boiling — C-4 had heat tabs beat, big-time — and Michael poured half the coffee into Snoopy's cup, which still had a little crust of last night's chop suey mixture. They ate quickly, and silently. Franks and beans. Hell of a way to start the day. He also had crackers and some peanut butter and jelly in this ration, and a can of fruit cocktail. Good.

"Don't, man," Snoopy said, when he started to open it. "Save it for when you need a treat. It's *gold,* man."

Michael thought about that, then put the can back in his rucksack. "A *'treat'*?" he said. "Sounds like girl talk to me."

Snoopy grinned. "Seemed like you enjoyed spending the night with me, babe."

"Loved it," Michael said, and ate peanut butter and crackers, while Snoopy made more coffee out of his ration packet, then refilled Michael's cup.

Their ration packets also held two pieces of gum, a packet of cocoa, sugar, salt, cream substitute, some toilet paper, and a very small pack of cigarettes. Lucky Strikes. He didn't smoke, but he was planning to start. Today.

"In your ammo can, r'else in the liner in your pot," Snoopy said, indicating his helmet.

"You don't wear one?" Michael asked, putting the cocoa, gum, and cigarettes in an ammo can, and the plastic-wrapped toilet paper inside his helmet liner, then gesturing towards Snoopy's boonie hat. Truth was, he kind of wanted a boonie hat himself, but he'd been too embarrassed to buy one at the PX in Chu Lai. Seemed like you ought to be *out* in the boonies, first, before you had the right to wear one. If he ever got near another PX though, he'd buy one for damned sure. By then, he probably would have earned it. In blood donated to mosquitoes alone.

Snoopy shrugged. "When we're lookin' for trouble, yeah. But, it's too damned hot."

"What about flak jackets?" They were pretty hot, too. And heavy. *Real* heavy. Not that he had taken his off yet, mind you. Didn't have any plans to do so in the near future, either.

Snoopy made a face. "L-T says we have to, when we're humpin'. He's real into going by the book."

Good. Then, he wouldn't look like a jerk for wearing one. Michael sipped some coffee. He had never been one to drink coffee, but this tasted great. "He okay? The lieutenant?" he asked.

Snoopy shrugged. "I guess so. Too gungy for *this* GI. Wants to be a captain so bad, he volunteers us for a lot of shit patrols."

Volunteering. His favorite thing.

A black guy who looked seventeen — *maybe* — came over to their foxhole. He moved quickly, both nervous and efficient, his eyes making him look a lot closer to seventy than seventeen.

"Hey, Doc," Snoopy said, and gestured with his cup. "Java, man?"

The guy, who was apparently the platoon's medic, shook his head, handing them each a small pill. "Y'all take these now, hear?" He looked at Michael. "They give you the big orange one, Monday last?"

Malaria pills. They had a weekly one, and daily ones. Michael nodded.

"Good," Doc said. "Don't care what you've

heard, you just take the damn things. Malaria here'll kill you quicker'n Charlie. And kill you *ugly*."

"The man is *already* ugly," Snoopy said.

Michael ignored him and took the pill. What he'd heard was, the malaria pills gave you diarrhea. His own observation was that this was true.

"You got plenty of salt tablets?" Doc asked.

Michael nodded.

"You take 'em regular," Doc said. "You don't, and we'll be evac'ing you out of here right quick. Don't drink all your water the first hour, either. We never got enough, and you gotta pace yourself."

Michael nodded. The salt pills, he'd heard, made you sick to your stomach. He could hardly wait to find out for himself.

Doc nodded too, looked worried, and moved on to the next foxhole, with his malaria pills.

"He's one of those join up, or go to jail guys," Snoopy said.

Michael looked after him, surprised. He'd met more than one guy like that during Basic — what better place to send a criminal than a war, where, hell, he could use his skills — but that kid looked like an altar boy. One you would *always* trust with the collection plate.

"He looks about twelve," he said.

"Think he's eighteen," Snoopy said. "Might be lying."

Didn't sound like Uncle Sam had spent much time checking.

"He's cool. Doesn't care if the whole NVA's firing at us," Snoopy went on. "You call for help, he'll show up. Doc Mendez in Three Squad's pretty good, but nowhere near as good as the real Doc here. He'll be poppin' away with the .45 with one hand, and patchin' you up with the other."

Michael kind of hoped not to see this in action. Like, just take Snoopy's word for it.

Around them, some of the guys were starting to bring in their claymores, empty their sand-bags, bury their C-rat cans.

"Get ready to saddle up," Sergeant Hanson said, behind them. "Got plenty of war out there waiting for us."

Great. Michael swallowed, and finished what was left of his coffee. Maybe it was just the ma-laria pill, kicking in quick, but he sure as hell felt sick to his stomach.

CHAPTER 7

SERGEANT HANSON came back over with some C-rations.

"Snoopy here'll tell you how to pack them," he said. "Make sure he's taped up, too, okay, Snoop?"

Snoopy nodded, already tearing open the boxes.

"Got some extra socks?" he asked.

Michael nodded.

"Okay." Snoopy took out a sock of his own to demonstrate. "Take what you want, put it in the sock, tie it to your ruck. We'll just bury up the rest." He glanced at the cans, then grinned. "Being as you're new and all, you wanna take the ham and limas?"

Michael looked at the boxes. Two ham and limas, one beef and potatoes, one meatballs and beans, two more franks and beans.

"I'll take *one* limas," he said. He could still taste the peanut butter, and was very tempted to drink one of his precious canteens. He was in no hurry to eat any more of it, that's for sure.

"No, don't," Snoopy said, as he started to throw the peanut butter away. "We run out of C-4, the peanut butter works *really* good, if you, like, put some bug juice with it, and fire it up."

Michael frowned at him. "No way."

"Yes, way," Snoopy said. "Pitiful as you are, you think I'd lie to you?"

Yes. Michael nodded.

"No way," Snoopy said. "I'm learning you jungle stuff and you should just find yourself real lucky, *I* think."

Michael frowned, but saved the peanut butter. There was also cheese spread and crackers. Sounded much better. "What were you, raised in the forest?" he asked.

"*Newark,* man," Snoopy said, as though there were no other possible place to be from on the face of the earth.

"Mostly stupid people come from there, right?" Michael said, saving the cigarettes, toilet paper, coffee, and sugar.

" 'Cept me," Snoopy said cheerfully.

Another fruit cocktail, a can of pound cake,

applesauce. Outstanding. Michael tied everything up in his extra socks, hefted them experi-
mentally, then tied them to the frame of his
rucksack.

"Not there," Snoopy said, and indicated the
straps on the rucksack. " 'Else they'll be banging
up your legs all day."

Michael thought about that, and retied his
socks.

Taping up involved jumping up and down to
see what rattled, then taping it down, or just
wrapping some tape around whatever the of-
fending object was to act as a cushion.

"The LRRPs worry helluva lot more 'bout
this," Snoopy said, "but Sarge likes us to do our
best."

LRRP was Long Range Reconnaissance Patrol — soldiers who went out into the jungle
alone, in very small squads, to get as close to the
enemy as possible, and gather intelligence. You
had to volunteer, and obviously he had no in-
tention of ever doing so.

Once the whole camp had been pretty well
taken apart, they all gathered around Lieutenant
Brady, who didn't look any more rested or clean-
shaven than he had the day before.

"1st Squad, you take point," he said. "2nd,

you're flank, 3rd, you bring up the rear. We'll be moving out in three. Remember, keep your intervals, and keep them on safety. 2nd and 3rd Platoons'll both be sweeping to the east. If there's trouble, we'll hook up."

1st Squad on point. Sounded like trouble already.

"J.D., you take point," Sergeant Hanson was saying, having gathered the 1st Squad around him. "And I want you on slack, Finnegan. Meat, you'll be next. I want you alert as you know how to be. They give you a signal, you pass it back. I want you looking left, and I want you looking alive."

Michael nodded.

"Snoopy, Viper, I want you behind me and Jankowski," Sergeant Hanson said. "Let's not set any records, okay? It's going to be triple-digits again."

They all nodded.

"Take it easy on the water, Meat — it has to last for a while," he said.

Michael nodded, self-consciously. Did he *look* like a screw-up, or was that standard advice for new guys?

"Okay." Sergeant Hanson turned to the rest

of the platoon. "Saddle up! And I want to see pots and jackets *on*."

There was a fair amount of grumbling, but they all put on their helmets and flak jackets — Michael careful not to fasten the helmet strap; they all hefted their rucksacks — Michael hoping no one could tell how much trouble he was having keeping his balance because of the weight; they checked their weapons, and their ammo, and the grenades hanging from their web gear. Then, they all moved out, J.D. in the lead. Even with his helmet on, that red hair made him easy to keep in sight.

The beginning, at least, was all downhill. Trails were much more likely to have booby traps, so they broke their own trail, which took much longer and was, Michael guessed, a hell of a lot noisier. Seemed loud to him, anyway. Every Viet Cong within miles must be able to hear them, tape or no tape. Sometimes, J.D. hacked away with a machete; sometimes, they were able to push through the bush without it. Crash, crackle, snap — either way.

"Intervals," Sergeant Hanson muttered somewhere behind him, after Michael caught a branch in the face for about the fifth time.

Meaning that he was walking too close to Finnegan. You were supposed to keep a decent-sized interval between you and the next guy so that one grenade, or one booby trap, or whatever, wouldn't blow away a whole bunch of guys at once. Michael nodded, and stayed a little further back, peering so hard to the left that it made his eyes hurt. Not that he, really, even knew what he was supposed to be looking for. And, Christ, he was perspiring so much that he had to keep blinking to keep his eyes clear.

J.D. stopped the column a few times, with a raised-arm signal, while he checked for booby traps. He found two, as they went along. One, a trip wire with a grenade attached to it, J.D. defused, everyone staying well back. This didn't do a whole lot to help Michael digest his breakfast. Probably didn't help J.D.'s stomach much, either. The other booby trap, more complicated, Lieutenant Brady and Sergeant Hanson — after some whispered conversation — decided to blow in place. Apparently, one of the guys in 3rd Squad had some EOD — Explosive Ordnance Disposal — experience. Even though Michael thought he had prepared himself for the sound of the explosion, and knew he was safely out of range, he still found himself ducking, instantly embarrassed, and hoping that no one else had noticed. But, some of the others had cringed, too. Too close for comfort. Not that anything about any of this was *comfortable*.

It was so hot that the air seemed to be moving in front of him. Of course, it *was* moving, what with all of the damned bugs. There were so many that it took effort not to inhale them. He wanted to slap them away, but knew that he couldn't, that he couldn't make noise, that he had to pay attention. To *everything*.

There were screeching noises — birds? monkeys? — and humming noises — the bugs, he figured. He had to keep staring into the jungle to his left, but it was hard not to watch his feet. Watch for booby traps. Every time a twig or a piece of bamboo or whatever would snap underneath someone's boot, he would flinch, his hand twitching against the safety of his gun, every muscle in his body tensing. Expecting the worst.

When they finally stopped for a break, sitting down in a loose defensive perimeter, he was so tired he almost fell over. He gulped about half of one of his canteens, taking two salt pills, too. Sergeant Hanson gave him a warning frown, and he nodded, putting the canteen away.

Most of the rest of the guys, after drinking some water, immediately started cleaning their guns, the firing and cam pins clenched between their teeth. You had to keep the barrel especially clean, or the stupid things jammed. Something you wanted to avoid at all costs. So, he cleaned his too, looking around nervously. It didn't take long — but what a hell of a time it would be to get attacked.

They moved out again. More thick, sweltering jungle, J.D. having to hack away at the bamboo, Finnegan moving up to help him. Michael felt dizzy from the heat, his mouth so dry that it felt as if he had been eating sand. The rucksack straps were cutting into his shoulders — slicing them, it felt like — and he kept shrugging, trying to knock the rucksack into a more comfortable position. Plus, his gear was so heavy that his back was killing him, and his legs were beginning to wobble. He stumbled a couple of times, and Finnegan frowned back at him. He nodded, struggling to regain his balance. Quietly.

What a nightmare.

Perspiring like a rush of faucets all over his body, he had to keep blinking. And blinking, the salt stinging his eyes. The M-16 didn't weigh much, but his arms felt tight and cramped, and he wanted to flex them. To stretch. To put the damned gun *down* for a minute. Hard to believe he could ever hate this war more than he already did.

The jungle thinned a little — for which he was very grateful — and he rubbed his sleeve across his eyes, trying to clear them. His hair felt soaking wet, and his helmet kept slipping down. He might need the strap just to keep the thing from falling off.

Suddenly, he heard popping noises. Little quiet cracks, and everyone else was hitting the dirt. So, he did too, a little late, the weight of his rucksack slamming him into the ground so hard that his face went into the moist ground. His breath was knocked out for a few seconds, then he managed to lift his head, spitting out dirt, trying to keep his body pressed low. Away from the bullets. Wishing for an instant foxhole to open up underneath him.

He couldn't see anything — any*one* — but everyone else was shooting, and if he didn't, they weren't going to like him much. They would think he was a coward. He *was*. But, he set the gun out in front of him and pulled the trigger.

The stupid thing wouldn't work. And he'd *just* cleaned it, for Christ's sakes. Panicking, he tried again, and again — and finally remembered to take off the safety catch. By the time he blew away his first magazine — a few seconds later — the rest of the shooting had stopped.

Not sure what to do, he started crawling forward, into the thick, thorny brush. Low-crawling was a lot harder with seventy pounds on your back than it had been on the course at Basic, but he couldn't stop — couldn't let them get away — couldn't be a coward — couldn't —

"The fuck you going, cherry?" Sergeant Hanson barked.

Michael stopped. He was alone. He was fifteen feet into the jungle, and he was all by himself.

"I'm going *after* them!" he said. Uncertainly.

"Let John Wayne go after 'em," Sergeant Hanson said, grimly. "*You* get back here."

Oh. He could barely crawl forward — how the hell was he going to crawl *backward*? Slowly, awkwardly, he pushed himself backwards, hearing his fatigues — and feeling his skin — tear on more than one thorn.

He could hear Lieutenant Brady's RTO, Manny, softly calling coordinates into his radio.

Apparently, air support was the next step. Or artillery.

"Just a sniper," Finnegan whispered, next to him. "He's didi-ed, but they'll put some rounds in, anyway."

Didi-ed? Michael nodded though, like he knew what the hell he meant. That the guy was gone, presumably.

Sergeant Hanson had them pull back a little, take cover, and the first round — white phosphorus, to use as a marker — came booming in. The Lieutenant made some corrections; then, another round — the real thing, this time — came pounding down into the tree line ahead of them. Lieutenant Brady corrected the coordinates again; artillery back at Firebase Joanne — wherever that was — adjusted and fired a few more rounds; then, it was over. Maybe it made a difference; maybe it didn't. And it was so loud that Michael couldn't not cover his ears, the ground shaking underneath him.

Welcome to the war. Again.

Sergeant Hanson crawled over next to him. "No more rock and roll, kid," he said. "You don't carry that much ammo. Keep it on semi, squeeze off a round at a time."

Michael nodded, somewhat sheepishly. Sergeant Hanson looked amused, patted him on the shoulder, and moved away.

They got underway again with surprisingly little fanfare, just plain picking themselves up and trudging along some more. Nothing but jungle; nothing but heat.

Michael was less nervous, though, figuring that he hadn't run away crying the first time they came under fire, so he was probably going to do okay. Not humiliate himself, anyway. Not that he cared what people thought, but — if they were going to think something, they might as well not think something bad.

The one thing they might think was that his ruck was too heavy for him. They would be right. He felt like he was trying to carry a sack of concrete *through* a brick wall.

He was beginning to stumble again, afraid that he wouldn't be able to make it another step, when — thank God — they stopped for another break.

Some of the others were opening C-ration cans, so, apparently, this was lunch. Other guys were just slouched on the ground, drinking water and looking exhausted. The last thing Michael wanted was food — his stomach still hurt from breakfast — but he should probably eat something, so he opened one of his cans of fruit cocktail. Heated to ninety or a hundred-something degrees, but nice and sweet. He took his time eating it, savoring every drop.

Snoopy, eating some cheese spread and crackers, sat next to him, looking amused. Looking terribly amused.

"*What*," Michael said finally.

"You're very, very pitiful," Snoopy said. "Cowboy."

"Yeah." Michael drank the syrup left in the can. "So?"

" 'Least you weren't crawling *away*," Snoopy said.

Michael nodded, and took out one of his little packs of Lucky Strikes — he also had a pack of Chesterfields — and looked at it. Studied it.

Snoopy watched him. "Bet you don't know how to smoke, either."

Michael nodded. He bet right.

"Pitiful," Snoopy said. "Just as pitiful as can be."

Michael nodded, and lit up. Other guys were smoking, so he figured they were allowed. American fighting forces, taking a break. Someone should tell the VC, maybe. Bear, who was sitting across the clearing, came over to sit on his other side. His uniform was dark with perspiration, and he looked as tired as Michael felt, but otherwise pretty cheerful.

"How ya doing, Mike?" he asked.

Michael shrugged. "Pretty hot."

"Hot as hell," Bear agreed, and stuck his hand out towards Snoopy. "Bear."

"Snoopy," Snoopy said, and they exchanged a complicated, soul-brother handshake. A dap, it was called, and it always made Michael feel sort of stupid and white and left-out.

So, he smoked his cigarette. Like the coffee, better than he had expected. The smoke made him cough a little, but — what the hell. He was in a war, he should be able to do whatever he wanted. Whenever he wanted.

"Took some fire," Bear observed, taking the olive drab towel from around his neck, and wiping his face.

Michael nodded, and smoked, managing not to cough this time. The smoke even seemed to discourage the bugs. A little.

"Sarge said I blew away too much ammo," Bear said, sounding kind of pleased with himself.

"Me, too," Michael said, and they both grinned.

"Don't get cocky," Sergeant Hanson said, drinking coffee with Viper a few feet away.

They both shook their heads. Then, they both grinned again.

CHAPTER 8

THE AFTERNOON was even hotter than the morning had been. It was hard to keep his mind on anything other than putting one foot down, and then putting the other foot down, and then, starting all over again. The heat seemed to come in waves, and they made him dizzy as hell.

One step. Another. Look left. Look *left*, for Christ's sakes. Everything was kind of swirling around, and he had to think even to remember which way left was. To remember what he was supposed to be doing. He heard a voice calling "Medic!", and when he turned to see who it was, the motion of doing so made him fall down.

There seemed to be people above him and he realized, dimly, that the medic was for him. That he was being turned over onto his back, and water was being splashed over his face.

"I'm all right," he said weakly. "Ground broke my fall."

"Come on, kid," Doc Adams said, trying to put something into his mouth. "Swallow these."

Michael swallowed, choked, then swallowed again.

"You all right, kid?" Doc asked.

He looked so damned young. "The fuck old are you, you call me 'kid'?" Michael asked, still choking a little.

"Shut up, troop," Doc said, and splashed some more water over his face. "I *told* you to take the damned salt pills."

"You have a couple more birthdays, *then* you call me 'kid,' " Michael said, and tried to sit up.

Doc got up. "He's fine," he said to Sergeant Hanson. "Give him another few in the shade here."

"Okay, Doc," Sergeant Hanson said. "Go check the other cherry, see if we're about to lose him, too."

Doc nodded, and went back down the column. Michael felt weak as hell, but also extremely stupid. Like a failure. Tough guys didn't let a little heat get to them. Damn. He also felt sick to his stomach, but he was embarrassed enough, without throwing up in front of everyone.

"How you doing, kid?" Sergeant Hanson asked, sitting next to him, looking pretty hot himself.

Michael had to blink a couple of times to be able to focus on him. "How old are *you*?"

Sergeant Hanson laughed, and opened his canteen, taking a gulp. "Shut up, kid."

There was something reassuring about that — you wouldn't tell someone who was dying of heat exhaustion to shut up — and Michael managed to push himself up to his elbows, looking around with a certain amount of confusion.

"Did I fall down?" he asked.

Sergeant Hanson laughed again. "Yeah, kid. You fell down."

"Hey, maybe he lost his memory," Snoopy said, and Michael realized that the whole squad was right around him. "Who won the pennant in 1948, Meat?"

"Fuck you," Finnegan said, instantly.

Snoopy grinned. "Oh — right. Y'all *lost* it that year."

"Lost it *big*," J.D. said. Drawled, really.

"Fuck both of you," Finnegan said, without much venom.

If he hadn't lost his memory, maybe he'd lost his mind, because this conversation made very little sense. "I wasn't even *born* in 1948," Michael said. "How'm I supposed to know?"

J.D.'s eyes widened. "It talks!"

"It's maybe going to live," Finnegan said.

"It's *very*, very pitiful," Snoopy said.

Sergeant Hanson put away his canteen. "You all right now, Meat?"

No. But, Michael nodded, and struggled to his feet.

"Okay," Sergeant Hanson said, and turned, motioning for the platoon to start moving forward again.

Which they did. Endlessly. The highlight of the afternoon was when they got to splash through a stream, pausing to dump water over their heads, and fill their canteens with muddy water. The low point, was the leeches they got. Michael managed to remember, before Sergeant Hanson had to tell him, that he had to put purification tablets into the canteens first, before he drank any. A lovely country. A lovely war.

They stopped for one more break, Michael too exhausted to do anything but sit in the shade, and cover his face with a still-damp towel. There was a hill up ahead, and apparently, they were going to climb it, and dig in for the night.

Uphill the rest of the way. Great.

It was the most tiring part of a very tiring day, climbing through brambly undergrowth, slipping and sliding when the going got steep. At least, climbing up steep grades seemed familiar to him. He just, usually, did it in below-freezing temperatures. When it was over a hundred degrees, and you were choking down salt tablets right and left, it was different. It made him curse every moment in his life that he had thought nice thoughts about mountains. About flights of stairs, even.

Everyone was tired as hell when they got to the top, but before anyone could sink down and relax, Lieutenant Brady had half of them guarding their new perimeter, and the rest of them digging trenches for the NDP.

No resupply today. No hot meals. No anything.

FTA, man. FTA.

Guarding was easier than digging — at least, it was with nothing happening — and Michael was glad that he had to guard first. When it was time to change places, a very grouchy Snoopy had carved a trench about a foot deep. They switched assignments without much conversation, and Michael started digging, each shovelful heavier than the one before.

Lieutenant Brady was going around checking fields of fire, and pointing out where he wanted each claymore mine set, with the trip flares beyond them.

"How you doing, Jennings?" he asked. "Heat get to you a little today?"

A little. "Yes, sir." They weren't supposed to say "sir" in the field, or do anything that might point out an officer to the enemy. Too tempting a target. "Uh, L-T," he corrected himself.

"Well, you may not believe it now, but you'll get used to it," Lieutenant Brady said.

He didn't believe it, but he nodded.

Lieutenant Brady nodded, too. "Carry on, then."

You didn't salute officers in the field, either, so Michael went back to digging.

It was almost dark by the time they were dug in. The word was, no night ambushes tonight because they were going to hook up with 2nd and 3rd Platoons the next day, and would resume ambushes then. Since 1st Squad had had to walk point all day, some guys from Two Squad went out on Listening Posts.

Fine. Michael was in no hurry to look for trouble. More trouble.

Almost everyone else was either eating, or

writing letters. Or rereading *old* letters. They said — they never really shut up, did they? — that you were supposed to burn any letters you got, after you read them, so they wouldn't get into enemy hands, but judging from the number of guys reading letters from the day before, it didn't look like anyone did.

If they were all writing letters, maybe he should, too. He could eat after it got dark. Not that he was hungry.

"Got any paper?" he asked Snoopy, who grunted, writing away, and handed him a sheet of light blue paper. Courtesy of the USO or the Red Cross, Michael was guessing. Unless Snoopy had real pastel sorts of tastes. "Thanks," he said. "Got a pen?"

Snoopy sighed deeply. "You know what I think?"

"Yeah," Michael said. "Got a pen?"

Snoopy pulled an extra ballpoint out of his rucksack. "You're very, very lucky you hooked up with me."

Michael nodded, and took the pen.

Okay, so now what.

Dear Mom and Dad, he wrote.

Okay. Now what.

Things are okay here.

Yeah. Having a wonderful time. Wish you were here. Forget the Rocky Mountains; *this* is a vacation paradise.

It's kind of hot.

Kind of. Like, passing-out hot. Like, he'd made a fool of himself today hot. Like he wasn't sure if he had lived it down yet.

The guys seem —

Like every guy everywhere, and like no guys he had ever met. What was the word for that? Began with "d"? Oh, hell, he wasn't a book guy. He should just use a word he knew.

— cool.

Oh, yeah, great word choice. Anyway. They seem like kids, and they seem like very tired old men. They make jokes, but they're very serious. They look —

Oh, hell, change the subject. Write about something cheerful. *Was* there anything cheerful?

Saw the ocean, it was really —

— cool.

— nice.

Yup, he was a writer guy, all right. Maybe he should write a goddamned *book*. Like — well, he wasn't a book guy, he wasn't going to remember writers' names.

Hemingway. Kind of a hard name to forget. Anyway.

The country is very pretty.

But sucks, big-time.

The people I've seen are very poor.

And the people he *hadn't* seen were killers. They might even all be the same people.

Change the subject.

There are mountains, but it's over 100 degrees, so I guess they don't ski much.

That was supposed to be a joke, only now that he'd written it, it looked stupid. But if he scribbled it out, they would think he was hiding something, and if he threw it away and asked for another piece of paper, Snoopy would probably smack him.

Of course, Snoopy wasn't very big, so it probably wouldn't hurt much.

Anyway.

Everything is very green.

Should he tell them about the mosquitoes? The screeching birds — or monkeys, or hyenas, or whatever they were? About the huge snake he'd seen slithering across a rotting log while they'd been stumbling around the jungle today?

And, what about the firefight? Thing is, he

kind of *wanted* to tell them. Wanted them to know. It hadn't been much, maybe, but it sure seemed that way to him, and he wanted to —

We had some contact today, only nothing really happened.

Except that he made a fool of himself.

No one got hurt.

On either side, he was guessing.

I hope all of you are fine. Don't worry, I'm fine too, just hot. Love, Mike.

He looked over what he had written, squinting in the fading light. Pretty stupid. Maybe he should —

"You don't even tell them about me?" Snoopy asked, reading over his shoulder.

Michael quickly turned the paper over. "It's private, okay?"

"Think I made a mistake," Snoopy said, turning the paper back over so he could finish reading it. "Should've called you Mr. Emotion."

Michael folded the paper up. "Got an envelope?"

"Wait a minute." Snoopy snatched the paper and pen away.

"Don't write anything," Michael said, trying to grab it back.

Snoopy ignored him, already scribbling. Michael sighed, waited for him to finish, then took the letter back.

We're keeping a real good eye on your son, it said. *He keeps begging us to call him "Meat," so we surely do. It's not kind of hot — it's* real *hot. Sincerely, PFC Robert Baker, 4/31, 196 LIB, 23rd Inf. Div.*

Snoopy had, surprisingly, very nice handwriting.

"Robert?" Michael said.

Snoopy nodded, taking out a can of beef and potatoes. "Didn't think my momma named me Snoopy, now did you?"

"Could be a family name," Michael said.

"Oh, yeah," Snoopy said, and cut off a chunk of C-4. "My dad *and* my grandad."

Right. Michael looked at his letter again. *P.S.,* he wrote at the bottom. *Pat Otis for me. We're supposed to stay away from the dogs here, in case they have rabies. Say hi to Dennis and Carrie.*

And tell Dennis to study, get good grades, go to college, and stay the hell *away* from this place.

On that happy note.

He took the envelope Snoopy had left out for him, folded the paper, and put it inside. He addressed it to his parents, put on his return address, then wrote "Free" in the corner where the stamp would ordinarily go.

One of the few benefits of being in the Army.

He would, however, be happy to give it up, and *pay* for the stupid stamps.

"Tell them to send some Kool-Aid," Snoopy suggested.

Good idea. Michael took the paper back out and wrote, *If you get a chance, could you send me some Kool-Aid? The water isn't very good. Thanks.*

He put the letter back in the envelope and sealed it up. It was going to be kind of hard to find a mailbox.

Okay, that was done. Now what.

"Gonna eat, man?" Snoopy asked, already digging into his beef and potatoes.

Why not. Nothing better to do.

If anyone had ever told him that war could be kind of — boring — he never would have believed it.

CHAPTER 9

Michael took out his can of ham and limas. Might as well get them out of the way. Save the meatballs and beans for tomorrow.

He could hardly wait.

Snoopy was heating water, and they split some cocoa. Weird. It was a million degrees out, they were a million miles away from anyplace normal, and they were drinking hot chocolate, like they were sitting in a lodge, their boots propped up near the fireplace, relaxing after a nice day on the black diamonds.

J.D. came wandering over, looking tired, eating a C-rat pecan nut roll. He nodded at both of them, and sat down on some sandbags, taking out one of his — very creased — pink letters.

"You did good today," Snoopy said.

J.D. shrugged. "Hate the point, man." His hair was light red under normal circumstances, but it looked very dark now — stiff and sticky with salt and perspiration.

"You did good though," Snoopy said, and Michael nodded. *He* couldn't imagine walking point, and being able to find actual booby traps.

J.D. shrugged again, took a sip of the hot chocolate Snoopy offered, then handed the cup back. "I'm too short for this shit," he said. "Walkin' 'round all day, going *no* place." He looked at Michael. "You okay now? You was looking mighty pale." He grinned.

"Lunch," Michael said, and shrugged. "Disagreed with me."

J.D. laughed, ran his hand through his hair, then frowned at his hand.

"Must be your shampoo," Snoopy said.

J.D. nodded. " 'R'else I gotta stop rinsing in oil drums."

"There you go," Snoopy agreed, and started heating up some more water.

J.D. took out a cigarette, looked at the dusky sky, shrugged, and lit up. Wasn't dark enough to worry about light discipline. Yet. "So." He looked at Meat. "Where you from?"

"Right outside Denver." He'd burned the bottom of his ham and limas, and they tasted even worse than they might have otherwise. "You?"

"He's a little corn-boy," Snoopy said. "Got husks coming out of his ears."

"Least *my* ears don't stick out," J.D. said, and looked at Meat. "Iowa. Place called Munterville."

Okay. Sure. He'd been there often.

"Near Ottumwa?" J.D. said.

Okay. Sure. Michael shrugged, and ate some scorched lima beans. Army food was a million times worse than high school cafeteria food. Which was pretty damned awful in its own right.

"And he can't hardly wait to get back and start plowin' those fields," Snoopy said cheerfully.

"What are *you* going to do?" J.D. asked. "Go home and hang out? Drink beer?"

Snoopy nodded. "I'm real good at that, yeah."

Michael was, too.

"Not me," J.D. said. "I'm going to go home, get Emily to marry me, then sit up on a tractor, happy as a pig in slops."

"How happy *is* that, exactly?" Snoopy asked.

"Happy as can be," J.D. said. "You got a girl, Meat?"

He'd *had* a girl. A girl who thought he was not just a ski bum, but a stupid, unambitious, regular bum, too. Not worth her time and trouble. Michael shook his head, and tossed away what was left of his ham and limas.

"Oh, no," Snoopy said. "You *ever* had a girl?"

"You got a lot to learn about privacy," Michael said, and lit a Lucky Strike. Smoking could grow on him. There was something emphatic and dramatic about it. Bogart.

Snoopy looked at J.D. "Guess that means no."

J.D. nodded.

"Okay, smart guy," Michael said. "*You* got a girl?"

"I got so many I cannot hardly keep track," Snoopy said. "And every one of them a beauty queen."

"You wish," Michael said, and let out some smoke. He had to learn how to blow rings.

"*You* wish," Snoopy said. "Girls all over the state'r crying themselves to sleep every night, praying for the day I get home, and am at their service again."

Michael shook his head. "No way, GI."

"That your friend? Going to let him go with you everywhere?" J.D. asked, indicating a leech visible through a tear in his t-shirt.

Oh, *fuck*. He thought he'd gotten them all.

"Boy needs a pet," Snoopy said, and he and J.D. laughed.

You weren't supposed to pull them off, because the heads would stay in your skin, and you'd get all infected. Some of the guys had used salt tablets, some of them had used bug juice, and the rest had tried to burn them off. Feeling sick, Michael made the tear a little wider, then held the end of his cigarette to the disgustingly bloated little thing, hearing a sizzle, and seeing a shrivel. Disgusting. Worse than ham and limas, even.

"Best check your nearest and dearest," J.D. advised. "That can be *real* unpleasant."

Michael instantly opened his fly. Preservation came *way* before modesty. All clear. Thank God. He redid his fly, shrugged his shoulders to loosen them, and tried to pretend he had not even had a *second* of panic. J.D. and Snoopy seemed to think it was all pretty funny.

Then again, they seemed to think that most things were pretty funny. Two of the Three Stooges.

And — speak of the devil — there was the Third. Finnegan came bopping over, carrying a small, battered transistor radio. Armed Forces Radio, playing "Mr. Tambourine Man." With surprisingly little static. Yes, it was war, and they were drinking hot — tepid, now — chocolate, and listening to rock and roll. Americans, gotta love them.

"Hey, boys," Finnegan said, and lay down with his head on his rolled-up flak jacket, his helmet over his eyes. His hair, naturally, still looked black, but there was some salt crusted in it.

"*This* guy," J.D. said to Meat, "is going to go home and be the toughest little cop in Boston."

"Second toughest," Finnegan said, without lifting his helmet. "My dad's the toughest."

Boston. Michael looked at Snoopy. "The Red Sox *lost* the pennant in 1948."

"Leave me alone," Finnegan said, not stirring otherwise.

Michael thought. "The Indians won?" he said.

Snoopy nodded. "Yup."

"Leave me alone," Finnegan said. "We won *this* year, didn't we? Of course, I was in goddamn *Vietnam* — but, we won it. I wait my whole life for them to win, and they up and do it the second I leave." Then, he sat up, looking at Michael, who noticed that he had "The Impossible Dream" written on his helmet. "Remind me to show you my Ted Williams ball."

Sounded like the punch line to a very dumb joke.

"It was only a foul ball — but *he* hit it," Finnegan said.

"And you caught it?" Michael asked. Politely.

"Well — I was eight," Finnegan said. "My dad caught it."

"Well, he's tough, your dad," Michael said, tried to blow a smoke ring, and failed.

The Doors, and "Light My Fire," came on.

"*Yes*," J.D. said, and turned it up.

Vietnam. The weirdest goddamn place in the world.

There was a moon that night, making it just light enough for Michael to be able to distinguish shapes while he was on watch. In a way, it was scarier to be *able* to see, than it had been staring into the blinding, pouring rain the night before. He could hear artillery off in the distance, enough of it to indicate that it was a support mission, and not just H & I. Oh, great. He thought he could hear gunfire too, but maybe he just *expected* to hear it.

His first watch was endless, but uneventful, and he was happy to curl into the dirt and let Snoopy take over, falling into an instant dreamless sleep.

When Snoopy woke him up, it seemed like

only about thirty seconds had passed. He had trouble remembering where he was, but then fumbled for his M-16 and his helmet, and got up. Snoopy was asleep almost instantly, too.

He was tired. He was real, real tired. He wouldn't drive a *car* in this condition, and they were expecting him to fight a war. Or *not* fight, if he was lucky.

It was hard to stay awake. The mosquitoes were swarming around, and he didn't put on as much bug juice as he probably needed because at least the annoyance of the mosquitoes would help keep him awake. He was already covered with bites, anyway. A lot of them looked more like *welts*. Itched like hell, too. So did the various cuts and scratches he had gotten today, and he also felt — pay attention. Pay attention.

He watched his fifty, or sixty, or whatever it was, meters worth of perimeter, letting his eyes sweep back and forth. But the rhythm of that got monotonous, and started to put him to sleep. So, he looked around in a darting, jerky kind of way, and it helped. A little.

What time was it? No, he shouldn't look — it would be too depressing. He had at least an hour and a half to go. Christ. Almost a *year* to go.

Then, there was a flash of bright light somewhere on the other side of the perimeter and, as
he heard claymores going off, he was wide-
awake. So was Snoopy, up and ready with his
gun. There was a lot of yelling, and now, a lot
of machine gun fire. M-16s, it sounded like —
were any of them AK-47s? VC? Who could tell
with all this noise?

"Do we go over there, or do we shoot here?"
Michael shouted, glancing from his section of
the perimeter to the chaos behind them — back
and forth, back and forth — wanting to do nothing more than pull his helmet down low and get
in the bottom of the foxhole.

"I don't know!" Snoopy shouted back, also
looking around wildly.

What?! "You're supposed to know what to
do!" Michael said. "I thought you knew everything!"

"I don't!" Snoopy said, holding an unarmed
grenade in one hand, the M-16 in the other,
clearly not sure what to do.

"What?!" Michael stared at him for a second,
then squeezed off about six rounds into the
dark — apparently empty — jungle ahead of
him. They shouldn't just *stand* — crouch —
here. It was so noisy, he couldn't tell if the rest

of the guys in his squad were shooting, too, or if it was just Three Squad, or what. He stopped firing, and looked back at Snoopy. "How long you been here?"

" 'Bout a month," Snoopy said.

Only a *month*? And he'd been acting like he knew every damned thing in the world? "You mangy son-of-a-bitch!" Michael said, and slugged him.

"Mangy?" Snoopy scrambled back up, dropping his gun. "Fuck you, *you're* mangy!" He swung wildly, his fist slamming into Michael's cheekbone, and then, they were struggling in the bottom of the foxhole, smacking the hell out of each other.

There was a firefight going on, and they were acting like eight-year-olds. Six-year-olds. It struck them both funny at about the same time, and they stopped fighting, panting and trying to get their breaths in the bottom of the foxhole.

"You *hit* me, you son-of-a-bitch," Snoopy said, breathing hard, and laughing a little.

"Because you're a *lying* son-of-a-bitch," Michael said, and he laughed, too.

They could hear the gunships swooping in, then, they could see the tracers — graceful and beautiful in the darkness, slicing dreamily to the ground. Michael had never seen anything quite like it, and he couldn't help watching. In fact, he suspected that his mouth was hanging open.

"The perimeter, man," Snoopy said. "We gotta watch."

Michael nodded, and turned to face the jungle as the helicopters came back on another strafing run. After that, some artillery rounds came in, the entire hill seeming to shake as they landed. Then, the barrage was over, and it was very quiet except for a few low voices. American voices, so Michael didn't worry. The voices sounded more irritated than panicked, anyway.

"I think you split my lip, man," Snoopy said, grumpily.

"Yeah, well, I can't even *see* out of my eye," Michael said, just as grumpy.

"You're a pitiful son-of-a-bitch," Snoopy said.

"So are you," Michael said, and they both watched the perimeter.

It was quiet the rest of the night — very quiet — but nobody got any more sleep, the entire platoon on full-alert. Sergeant Hanson was by to check on them, make sure that everything was all right.

"What happened, Sarge?" Snoopy asked.

"Washington said he saw something," Sergeant Hanson said. "We'll probably go out there in the morning and find a monkey, but . . . Stay alert, okay, guys? Anything happens, claymores and grenades first."

They both nodded, and he was gone.

"I should've thrown a grenade," Michael said.

"I should have done *something*," Snoopy said.

Michael shrugged. "I didn't see anything."

"I didn't, either," Snoopy said.

They watched the jungle. Michael's eye hurt. He'd taken a couple in the mouth, too.

"So, do you know *anything*?" he asked.

"I know pretty much," Snoopy said, without much confidence. "Mostly, I ask Viper and J.D."

"Great," Michael said.

"Not that I can't teach *your* sorry ass a few tricks," Snoopy said.

"You're the one bleeding," Michael said.

They were quiet for a minute.

"Mangy," Snoopy said, and shook his head.

As soon as it was light out, Lieutenant Brady sent out a small patrol, but all they found were a couple of blood trails. Presumably human, presumably the enemy. Lions and tigers and bears, oh, my. When it came to body counts, though, blood trails were considered good enough, so the Lieutenant seemed pleased. Contact, enemy kills, no friendly casualties. An officer's dream come true.

Michael and Snoopy, both clumsy with fatigue, made some coffee. Heavy on the sugar and cream substitute.

"I'm not hungry," Snoopy said.

"Neither am I," Michael said.

Snoopy split the coffee between their two cups. "You look like shit, man."

Michael drank some. His eye hurt. "*You* look like you ran into Marciano."

"You wish," Snoopy said. "Want to split one of the franks and beans?"

Michael shrugged, and Snoopy nodded, heating it up.

Sergeant Hanson came over, stopping when he saw them in the light. "What the hell happened here?" he asked, hands on his hips.

Would you believe — the Viet Cong? Michael shrugged, and ate a spoonful of franks and beans.

"Ran into a wall," Snoopy said.

Sergeant Hanson frowned at him, then frowned at Michael.

"With me, it was a mantelpiece," Michael said.

Neither of these explanations went over real big.

"There a problem here?" Sergeant Hanson asked, looking about as royally pissed as someone could look.

They shook their heads.

"There's a problem, I want to know about it," he said. "I don't want to get *my* shit blown away because *you* two think you're still in junior high."

"No problem," Snoopy said.

"No problem at all," Michael said, and ate some more of their communal franks and beans. Scorched again.

"There better not be," Sergeant Hanson said. "I see anything I don't like today, and one of you'll be switched out of this squad."

They both nodded.

"We move out of here in twenty minutes," he said.

They both nodded.

"He's pissed," Snoopy said, as Hanson strode away.

"Royally," Michael said, and they continued their breakfast.

CHAPTER 10

IT WAS HOT. It was hot. It was hot. Michael managed not to pass out, but one of the guys in 2nd Squad — not Bear — wasn't so lucky, and the L-T had to call in a medevac. And everyone got even hotter, trying to blast and chop out an LZ big enough for the chopper to get in.

The guy looked terrible — very pale and still — but Michael couldn't help being envious as the helicopter took off, taking him out of the jungle and back to Chu Lai, and — relative — civilization. Lucky son-of-a-bitch.

Lieutenant Brady was checking his map, so Michael sat down, drinking some water — he had to be careful, he was starting to run low — and taking another salt tablet. He was sitting with the rest of the squad, but Sergeant Hanson motioned him over with a quick movement of his eyes.

Odds were, he was going to get yelled at some more. Everyone had noticed — it was hard to miss — that he and Snoopy both looked pretty messed up, and they had been the butt of more than a few jokes. Doc had checked his eye, told him he was a stupid kid, and then put some kind of antiseptic on Snoopy's lip, telling him that he was a stupid kid, too.

Anyway. He walked over to Sergeant Hanson, who had one eye on the terrain around them. Sergeant Hanson was *always* alert, always watching. As far as Michael could tell, anything Hanson missed, wasn't worth seeing.

He glanced at Michael, before looking back at the jungle. "I want to hear what really happened."

"It was nothing," Michael said. "It was no big deal."

Sergeant Hanson gave him a quick — but definite — frown. "Was it a race thing?" he asked.

What? Michael looked at him blankly.

"Because," now, he was looking right at him, "that is one particular kind of shit I don't put up with."

"It *wasn't*," Michael said. Better not seem like he was protesting too much. "It was just a misunderstanding."

Sergeant Hanson looked at him. He didn't look friendly. "I know Snoopy — I don't know you. Talk to me."

Michael sighed. Oh, all *right*. It was going to sound stupid though. Hell, it *was* stupid. "I, uh — he kind of led me to believe — I thought he'd been here forever and knew what the hell he was doing, and I was mad when I found out he didn't." He frowned. Did that come out right? "Hadn't been," he added, uncertainly. "Doesn't."

"Snoopy's no fool," Sergeant Hanson said, still not friendly.

"I'm not saying he is," Michael said quickly. "I just — it was kind of a heat of the moment thing, Sarge."

Hanson looked at him, expressionless.

"For Christ's sakes," Michael said. "Would we share our damn breakfast if we hated each other? Back off, why don't you?"

"Hey, I outrank you, kid," Sergeant Hanson said, "and no matter where we are, you best remember the chain of — "

"So, bust me," Michael said. "Send me to LBJ. Send me to *Leavenworth,* for all I care."

Sergeant Hanson shook his head. "No, you're

a scrapper. We need scrappers out here." He frowned. "I *like* scrappers."

"I, um — " Michael frowned, too. "I have a little bit of a temper sometimes."

Sergeant Hanson nodded. "I've noticed that about you," he said, and smiled, which suddenly made him look a whole lot younger, and a whole lot sweeter.

Oh. "Sarge?" This was probably a mistake, but — he was curious. "How old are you, Sarge?"

Sergeant Hanson didn't answer right away, his eyes sweeping the jungle. "Be twenty-one in April," he said, finally.

Really? "That's *all*?" Michael said.

"Yeah." Hanson frowned at him. "How old are *you*?"

Okay, that was fair enough. "Be nineteen, the end of January," Michael said.

They looked at each other, suspiciously.

"Not too many shopping days left," Michael said, and Sergeant Hanson laughed.

"Okay, Meat," he said. "I guess you get the last word."

Oh, good. He almost never got the last word. Michael nodded, and went back to sit with the others.

Snoopy grabbed his arm, examined it carefully, then dropped it. "Don't see *too* many chew marks," he said.

"That's 'cause he spit me out right away," Michael said.

Snoopy nodded. "White meat. Nobody *I* know, likes white meat."

Everybody but Viper — who was checking the inside of the barrel on his M-60, and looking vaguely amused by this — frowned at him.

Snoopy looked innocent. "What?"

"Saddle up!" Sergeant Hanson said, and damn near everyone groaned. Then, helmets and flak jackets went back on, canteens were put away, and everyone got up.

Time to go back to the war.

They walked. And they walked. And they walked. It was like walking through a steam bath, Michael feeling so much perspiration that his fatigues were actually heavy. Out of the hills, through a bamboo thicket — hot, hot, hot, hot — and then, into rice paddies. The first ones Michael had walked through. They were beautiful, and green, and laid out in large neat squares. Sort of like graph paper.

Not that he was a math guy.

There were dike things separating the paddies, but the theory was that they were the most likely spot for mines. That Charlie — Charles; Chuck; the faceless enemy, who might or might not be out there — assumed Americans would be lazy and take the easy way. Probably not a bad assumption, sometimes. Maybe even often.

But not 1st Platoon. They took the hard way, plowing through the water. It was slower, and it was noisier, but — in theory, again — it was safer. Michael found it hard to walk, holding his gun up high to try and keep it from getting wet, the muddy bottom of the paddies sucking at his boots. The mud was so deep, he would sink in practically up to his knees. Plus, he felt so damn — exposed. So far, he'd only walked in jungle, and on hills. Being out in the open like this was scary.

At one point, there was some shooting, and everyone slammed down into the water — *under* the water, if possible — trying to keep their guns up. They were *supposed* to work if they got wet, but why take chances? Michael wasn't even sure where the fire had come from, but when everyone else started shooting back, he did, too, running through one clip, then slamming in another, and running through that.

Rock and roll, here to stay.

It started, and ended, so quickly that he didn't even really have time to be scared. And he still wasn't quite sure what was going on.

The gunships came in and fired at the tree line for a while; then, it was quiet; then, they all got up. The palm trees in the tree line were shot up some, but they were still pretty.

Part of him was scared — expecting raging gunfire any second, but the rest of him was so hot and tired and wet that it was hard to feel much of anything. Even fear. The sniping seemed so — random. And the shooting back — at nothing he could see — just seemed pointless.

Finally, they climbed up out of the paddies, into a small thicket of trees. There were hedgerows — *hedges?* in Vietnam? like it was a normal place? weird — beyond them, and he could see the tops of some little thatched huts that looked like something out of *National Geographic*.

A village. Okay, *now*, he was scared.

The word passed quietly — they were supposed to take a few minutes to rest up, then be prepared to sweep through the village. Apparently, 2nd and 3rd Platoons were set up in an ambush perimeter on the other side of the village. So, they were supposed to sweep through, and if there was any trouble, just drive it towards the waiting ambush.

Search and Destroy. With the emphasis on the search, or on the destroy? Either way, it sounded like trouble.

Michael drank some water, burned off a couple of leeches, slapped away some biting red ants — stung like hell — and waited for the order to "Saddle up!" Already, his least favorite two words in the English language.

The call came, all too soon, and they were moving out. Slowly, through the thicket, through the hedgerows, through tall sharp grass and into the village. Slowly. Very slowly.

There were about twelve little huts, a couple of rickety wooden pens with skinny chickens and a pig, a battered wooden well, a building that looked sort of like a primitive church. A lot of empty-eyed children came running out, kind of swarming around. There were women, who didn't even look up from underneath those scary conical hats, and a couple of old men, feebly doing chores. These people didn't look dangerous; they looked *pathetic*. Poor, and beaten down.

And it smelled awful. No septic tanks around *here*.

The platoon fanned out slowly through the village, looking around. Something grabbed Michael's pants leg, and he flinched, clutching at his gun.

A child. A very small and filthy child. A boy.

"Chop-chop, GI," the little boy said, yanking at his leg.

What was that, a threat? Michael moved uneasily past him.

"Chop-chop!" the little boy said. "GI, numbah one!"

Michael looked at Snoopy. "The fuck's he want?" he asked, uneasily.

"Food, man." Snoopy took out the remaining can of ham and limas, and flipped it to the little boy, who ran away with it, into a hut.

Oh. Michael swallowed, tightly gripping his gun. He *liked* children. He could be sort of a grouch sometimes — no, really? — and none of the other ski patrol guys could figure out why he never bitched when he had to teach the toddler ski classes. But — he liked it. He liked *them*. Cute as hell, always real determined, always real happy. In another country, these kids would probably be happy, too.

Snoopy gave him a little whistle, standing outside a hut, and Michael went over to join him.

"Come on," Snoopy said, and stepped cautiously inside.

There was a very frail woman — not that he had ever seen a *large* Vietnamese person — doing something with rice. Making it into balls, looked like. Weird. She and the little girl sitting in the corner didn't say anything. Didn't even really look up, heads bent under hats.

"I don't like this," Michael said, as they looked around.

Snoopy shrugged, sticking his gun into a jar of rice and moving it around.

"It's their *house,*" Michael said. "It's rude."

"No shit," Snoopy said, jabbing his gun at a mat on the floor, then into the woven-leaf walls.

"So, cut it out," Michael said, as Snoopy kicked some baskets out of the way, more rice and some dried fish spilling out of them. "You don't have to wreck stuff."

Snoopy stopped long enough to scowl at him. "Far as I can figure, everyone in this damned country is VC — so we can do whatever we have to do to find 'em."

Michael scowled back. "Yeah, well, you're scaring the hell out of that little kid."

Snoopy looked over at the little girl, who was watching them now, her eyes huge. "Yeah, she's probably scared 'cause she's sitting on a buncha grenades." He motioned roughly with his gun for her to get up.

Michael shoved him. "Act *decent,* why don't you!"

"*You* act decent," Snoopy said. "*I* want to get out of this place alive."

"Fine," Michael said, and they finished the search in silence.

They left the place in a mess, a lot of things knocked over and spilled, and Michael felt terrible.

"Excuse me," he said to the woman, who was still at the small table with her rice bowl. He gestured around. "Number ten — I'm sorry." Number one was slang for "the best," and "number ten" was slang for "the worst." There was no in-between.

He apologized again, but the woman never looked up.

"You know better," he said, grimly, to Snoopy as they went outside.

"Yup," Snoopy said. "And when you know better, you won't feel sorry for 'em either."

Michael just shook his head, and looked away. He saw a little bony dog cowering near the pigpen, and couldn't stop himself from walking over. He crouched down, holding out his left hand, the stock of his gun resting in his right.

"Hey, pup," he said. "Come here, pup."

The dog shivered, pressing against the splintery wood.

"Good dog, come on." Michael snapped his fingers lightly. "Come here." He'd probably get grief for this, but — he took out his peanut butter and jelly and crackers, opened it, and held out a cracker. "Come here, pal."

The dog took one tentative step, his ratty little tail giving an even more tentative wave.

"That's right," Michael said. "Good boy."

The dog took another step, then suddenly lunged, snatching the cracker out of his hand, almost biting him. Then, he cringed away.

"That's okay," Michael said, and took out another cracker. "Good dog."

The dog, obviously starving, swallowed the cracker in one gulp, but let Michael pat him this time. It trembled, and Michael could feel every single rib, but — it was nice to pat a dog. Made him feel human. The dog wagged its tail, less tentatively, and he felt even better.

Then, he heard a voice behind him. "What the hell are you doing, Jennings?"

Lieutenant Brady. What did it *look* like he was

doing? "I'm winning his heart and mind, sir," Michael said, and kept patting the dog.

Lieutenant Brady's expression twitched a little. Mad, or trying not to laugh? Did it matter, really? In the scheme of things?

"Jennings," he said, sounding patient. "We all like dogs. But, that's not why we're here. Leave it, and fall in with the others."

Michael nodded, gave the dog the last of the crackers, patted him one more time, then got up. If only he could spend the rest of his tour just sitting here, patting this dog. Poor little thing.

"L-T!" a voice called, and Lieutenant Brady hustled over to where a couple of guys from Three Squad were standing, next to a large tuft of grass.

They had found, it developed, a tunnel. No one had found anything else — no weapons, no ammo, no anything — but this was clear evidence that the VC had been around here somewhere. That they were maybe still around. People had found a lot of rice, too — more than seemed necessary for a village this size — but, who the hell knew? Maybe they'd just — harvested, or something.

There was a debate over whether they should send someone down into the tunnel, or just blow the thing and leave it at that. Michael wished like hell, during all of this, that he could find the dog and pat him some more.

It was decided, finally, to blow the tunnel, so someone shouted, "Fire in the hole!", tossed in a couple of grenades, and everyone else ducked. Then, Fish, the guy who knew EOD from Three Squad, wired the hole up with some more serious explosives, detonated them, and the ground shook and caved in.

Some of the villagers looked scared; most didn't look anything at all. Michael handed his peanut butter and jelly to the nearest person — an old woman, then fell in with the others. He could hear some laughing, near one of the huts, and saw some children getting their share of amusement out of watching J.D. and Finnegan do the Mexican Hat Dance around someone's conical hat. The children, in a sort of stilted way, seemed to find this hilarious.

Lieutenant Brady did not. "What the hell are you two doing?" he asked, striding over.

They stopped dancing, looking very serious.

"The Vietnamese Hat Dance, sir," J.D. said, solemn as can be.

Finnegan nodded. "Ancient ritual. Think we can break the heat wave."

"Maybe even end the war," J.D. said.

"Well, cut it out," Lieutenant Brady said, and motioned his RTO over, so he could call the results of the sweep into HQ. And, presumably, find out what to do next.

More hurrying up and waiting.

"Dinky-dau," Finnegan said, motioning to Lieutenant Brady, and most of the children giggled. By the way he twirled his finger beside his head, "dinky-dau" must mean something akin to "loco." Instead of giving them Nine Rules when they came in-country, it would make a hell of a lot more sense to give them language lessons. All of this would be a lot less complicated if they could understand each other.

He was starting to sound like some damned book guy.

Where was the dog, anyway? He looked around.

Out of nowhere, there was an explosion, then, a shout, and everyone snapped into defensive position, looking for cover and to see where it had come from. Michael followed the screams and saw a guy from Two Squad, lying on the ground, holding what was left of his right arm. Jesus.

A mine. Judging from the rice, and basket

pieces, strewn around him, the guy had checked a basket outside one of the huts, and it had blown the hell out of him. The guy was screaming his head off, Doc was over there slapping on a tourniquet, and everyone else was swearing and swinging their guns around, waiting for the right emotional trigger to set them off.

"No VC, no VC," one of the old men was saying, his voice high and panicky.

Manny, the L-T's RTO, was calling in for an urgent dust-off, giving the coordinates.

"No VC, no VC!" the old man kept saying, the high pitch of his voice more grating and upsetting than the guy lying screaming on the ground with blood sprayed all over him. Almost.

"Shut up," someone said, and knocked the old man over.

"Yeah." Another guy got ready to kick him. "Shut up."

"Okay, okay." Sergeant Hanson appeared, leaving Doc and the screaming guy, whose screams were starting to fade to a "Don't leave me, Doc, don't let me die," over and over. "Take it easy, boys," Hanson said, very calm. "Everyone, just take it easy. Let's secure an LZ over there — " he pointed to a spot near the edge of the village, beyond which 2nd and 3rd Platoons were supposed to be waiting, well out of the way of all of this — "and get ready to pop some smoke."

"But, Ace, man," someone protested. "They got Ace, Sarge."

"Right," Sergeant Hanson said, very calm. "Now let's do what we can to help him get out of here, and get back to the World. Move it!"

Everyone moved it, slowly, the edge of violence still strong in the air, Michael completely unnerved by it. There was a lot of low grumbling, but they did what Sergeant Hanson said.

"*Told* you we can't trust these fuckers," Snoopy said, next to him, his expression so dark and angry that he was almost unrecognizable. "Can't trust 'em at all."

Michael nodded, reluctantly, and followed the others to the LZ.

CHAPTER
11

DURING THE ENTIRE TIME that they waited for
the dust-off, standing guard, nobody spoke, except for occasional bitter mutters. The helicopter
came in, without receiving any fire, and pulled
out, without anyone saying a word. No one even
really looked at anyone else. 2nd Platoon had
come into the village now, with 3rd Platoon
maintaining security out in the jungle. Lieutenant
Brady was conferring with the lieutenant in
charge of 2nd Platoon, and when they were finished, they both looked very grim. Lieutenant
Brady stepped away, motioned his squad leaders
over, and they all talked briefly, too.

"What's going on?" Michael asked.

Jankowski, standing near him, hunched from
the weight of the PRC-25 radio, shrugged. "Deciding should we torch the place."

"But — they live here," Michael said.

"Don't be such a goddamn cherry," Jankowski said, and moved away from him.

When Sergeant Hanson came over, he looked very serious.

"Okay," he said quietly. "Do it."

"What about the people?" Michael asked, as the rest of 1st Platoon moved, kind of like tired robots, to start burning the village, the angry energy of a few minutes before having been replaced by a kind of resigned exhaustion.

"Just do it," Sergeant Hanson said. "It comes straight from the CO."

Burn someone's house down? "But — where do they — " Michael stopped. "What happens to them?" He could see 2nd Platoon assembling the villagers, starting to lead them away. "Where are they going?"

Sergeant Hanson looked much too tired to argue. "Just *do* it," he said.

Destroy the village? Fuck that. Michael folded his arms, and stayed right where he was.

"They get relocated, Meat," J.D. said, his voice as low as everyone else's was. "It's *procedure,* when they're VC sympathizers. Happens all the time." He had a cigarette hanging out of his mouth, apparently too tired to use his hands to smoke it. "You'll get used to it."

Not likely.

No one looked very happy about burning the village, but they were doing it — Search and Destroy, all right — and as Michael stood there, knowing that he should, first and foremost, be worried about the people, who were being taken off to some collection point somewhere, on their way to some refugee camp, but more than anything, deep inside, he was worried about what was going to happen to the dog.

When they were finished with the village, they had another klick — kilometer — or so to get to their probable NDP and, once again, it was all uphill. It was going to be much bigger tonight, with 2nd and 3rd Platoons setting up camp with them. All of Echo Company, except for 4th Platoon — weapons — which was off at the firebase, pulling security.

The hump was slow and exhausting, but otherwise without significant incident — other than the fact that someone saw a snake, panicked, and shot the hell out of it. When they got to the NDP, Michael — tired as he was — had a lot of angry energy to burn, and so he took the first turn digging. Snoopy didn't argue. Didn't say much of anything, actually. Neither of them did. Wasn't much *to* say.

There were a lot of roots, then hard red clay. And Michael was happy to put his back into digging it out. Then, he was happy to go pull guard. By himself.

His squad was going out on night ambush, but they wouldn't be leaving until after dark. When it came to that pre-twilight time, when everyone smoked and ate and wrote letters and all, he wasn't sure what to do. He didn't feel like talking to anyone. He didn't feel like being within a million miles of this place, or with these people. Being a part of any of this. So, he sat a ways away, his rifle across his lap, looking down the hill at the jungle.

Snoopy came over. "You gonna eat?"

"No," Michael said, not looking at him. "I'm kind of tired."

"You're gonna wish you had," Snoopy said. "When we get out there tonight."

Michael shrugged, breaking down the M-16 so he could clean it.

"Whatever," Snoopy said, stiffly, and walked away.

He had been sitting there for a while, his weapon cleaned and reassembled twice, when someone sat next to him. Jesus, the guy was incapable of taking a hint. He looked up in extreme irritation — and was surprised to see that it was Lieutenant Brady. He was real skinny, the Lieutenant was — especially up close. One of those guys who even if he *did* shave, looked like he hadn't — very dark hair, very pale skin.

"First ambush tonight," he said.

Michael nodded.

"Hanson'll take care of you," Brady said. "He's one of the best."

Michael nodded.

They sat there for a minute, Brady lighting up a cigarette and offering Michael one, which he accepted.

"So," Lieutenant Brady said, and looked at him.

"Things were getting out of control there today, sir," Michael said, and looked back at him.

Lieutenant Brady sighed. "SOP. That's our *job*. That's why we're here."

Michael let out some smoke. "Felt like a Nazi, sir." Not that officers appreciated honesty, as a rule.

Lieutenant Brady sighed even more deeply. "It's a complicated war, Jennings. We're all just doing our best."

Michael didn't say anything.

"You and I are just part of the machine," Lieutenant Brady said.

Michael shrugged. "Doesn't make it right, sir."

"Look — " Lieutenant Brady stopped. "What's your first name again? Michael?"

Michael nodded.

"You're going to do so many wrong things in the next year, Michael — God willing — that it's going to be hard to — " He stopped again. "Well."

They smoked.

"Your 201 — " Army personnel file " — is pretty mixed," Lieutenant Brady said, and glanced at him.

Michael shrugged. "Don't want to be here."

Lieutenant Brady nodded.

Being this honest wasn't going to get him all that great a reputation, but — hell with it. "I, uh — I'm having trouble understanding what's going on," Michael said. "It seems — I don't know."

Lieutenant Brady didn't answer right away. "The bottom line," he said, after a pause, "out here, is that we all have to be able to depend on each other. You have to be able to live with yourself, but the group is more important. Not everything you do is going to be right, but most of the time, you aren't going to have the luxury of stopping to figure that out."

Sounded like he was talking to both of them, maybe.

They sat there.

"Did you volunteer for this?" Michael asked. "Sir?"

Lieutenant Brady sighed. "I grew up military. It's — what the men in my family do."

Didn't sound like this man was all that thrilled about the family business.

"You're good on the hills," Lieutenant Brady said, abruptly changing the subject. "I *expect* the new guys not to be able to keep up, the first couple of weeks."

"I've had a lot of practice," Michael said. "Climbing."

Lieutenant Brady looked over. "You a country boy?"

Michael shook his head. "Ski patrol."

Now, Lieutenant Brady *really* looked at him — like he was a person, instead of just another soldier. "Seriously?"

Michael nodded.

"I'll be damned." Lieutenant Brady laughed. "That's a new one."

Michael shrugged, and took a drag of his cigarette.

"I've never tried that," Lieutenant Brady said. "Skiing."

"It's the greatest," Michael said, feeling very far away just thinking about it. Feeling — as close as he ever got to enthusiasm. "It feels — clean. Feels like you're flying."

"Hunh," Lieutenant Brady said. "I ever get out of here, maybe I'll give it a try."

Michael nodded.

They sat there for another minute.

"I play the piano," Lieutenant Brady said, unexpectedly, then looked a little embarrassed. "I — really like it."

"You good?" Michael asked.

Lieutenant Brady thought about that. "I don't know. Never had time to find out."

Michael nodded, and they sat there.

"Well." Lieutenant Brady stood up, clearly

still embarrassed. "You take care of yourself, Michael. Keep an even keel."

"Yes, sir," Michael said, and was surprised to find himself sorry to see him go. He wasn't a talk-to-officers kind of guy. He wasn't even a *talking* guy, for Christ's sakes.

It was almost dark. He was hungry. Slowly, he stood up, every muscle stiff and achy, and walked over to his foxhole, where Snoopy, J.D., Finnegan, and Jankowski were sitting. Viper, as generally seemed to be true, was off somewhere by himself, cleaning his M-60.

"Want some coffee, guy?" Snoopy asked.

Michael nodded, sitting down.

"We were talking 'bout how Snoopy doesn't have a girl, never has, and never will," Finnegan said, his mouth full of franks and beans.

"*Doesn't* have a girl?" Snoopy said, handing Michael his cup. "I got so many, it'd make you sick."

"No way," J.D. said. "Marilyn Monroe could be lying here, waiting for you, and you wouldn't know what to do."

"Well, no," Snoopy said, drinking some coffee as Michael handed the cup back. "Not in front of y'all. Because — that would be weird."

"You're not man enough, anyway," J.D. said. "You're not even *boy* enough. Guys see *you* in the locker room, they're laughing like to die."

"You wish, pale-boy," Snoopy said.

"Hey, I *know* what *I'm* talking about," J.D. said, and tapped the pocket where he kept his letters.

"Oh, no," Finnegan said to Jankowski. "We're about to have to hear about Emily again."

Jankowski nodded. "I bet she's fat. I bet she's big as a house."

"Bet she makes *bulldogs* look real cute," Finnegan agreed. "I bet — "

"You're jealous," J.D. said. "You just wish you had it as good as me."

"One look at *me*," Snoopy said, "and it'd be, good-bye, dumb potato-picker."

"Corn," J.D. said. "We grow corn. Besides, she sees *your* ugly face, she'll be sick for a week."

"She'll be *celebrating* for a week," Snoopy said. "That's 'bout all *I* know."

Guy talk. Almost always stupid, almost always amusing. Michael shook his head, and took out a can of C-rations. He might not feel like participating — nothing new there, really — but it was funny as hell to listen.

Made the day fade a little.
Not enough.

They got ready to move out on night ambush around 2100. A few guys from 2nd Squad were coming along, so that there were ten of them altogether. They didn't bring all that much — ammo, frag grenades, flares, claymores, canteens, their ponchos. Every other guy carried an entrenching tool. Sergeant Hanson had a starlight scope — looked sort of like a periscope, and when you peered through it, night was supposed to be as clear as day, although very green. The only time he'd ever used one was on night maneuvers during AIT. And he only got a couple of minutes with it.

They could wear flak jackets if they wanted — Michael wanted to — but helmets weren't recommended. Too cumbersome, making it hard to see. Most of the guys wore boonie hats; Michael had to get one. *Soon*. Even though his uniform was pretty filthy and getting torn up, it was still damned obvious he was a new guy. A very nervous new guy, although he tried his best to look cool. Calm. And collected.

Sergeant Hanson checked everyone — made sure they had everything he wanted them to

bring, made sure anything that might make noise
was taped down, or even discarded. Once they
were out there, they would be on complete noise
discipline — light discipline was taken for
granted — no cigarettes, in other words — and
unless there was an extreme emergency, Jankowski wouldn't even speak over his radio. He
would just click the handset twice every hour on
the hour to let Lieutenant Brady and the rest
of the CP know they were okay. At best, he
might whisper "Sit-rep negative," and leave it
at that. A sit-rep was a situation report. Pretty
self-explanatory.

They were going out to some trail junction,
not even a klick away, where they would set up,
and wait for the enemy to walk by. Maybe. As
they left, no one said good-bye or even really
looked at them.

Encouraging.

It was raining lightly, and the going was slippery. J.D. was on point — as always — and he
set a very slow pace. It was so dark that they
couldn't be more than a few feet away from each
other, or they would get separated.

A nightmare Michael didn't even want to
think about.

He didn't even know the guy walking in front

of him, but as they moved around slippery twists and turns, vines and branches thick around them, he leaned forward enough to touch the guy's rucksack. Make sure he was still there. Snoopy, behind him, did the same thing a couple of times, and once, it knocked him off balance. He wasn't the only one who was tripping, more than occasionally.

It took forever, and to him, they seemed very noisy. The ground was muddy, and would make a sucking sound every time a boot left it, and most of them were loudly out of breath. Sometimes, he'd hear a little equipment clink, too. Maybe the rain muffled the sounds though. He hoped.

And, truth was, it was so dark, he just plain closed his eyes a few times and kept his hand on the ruck in front of him because he couldn't bear to look around. Hated not being able to see anything. Even though he could hear distant artillery, and some machine-gun fire, *way* off, it felt like they were the only people in the world. Alone, and in the dark.

When they got to wherever it was they were supposed to be, Sergeant Hanson moved up from the back of the column, and set each pair of guys where he wanted them, all about ten or fifteen meters off the main trail, in thick bush. They were going to set up in an L-ambush, which looked exactly the way it sounded. The idea was to trap the enemy in the middle, where they would take fire from two different directions, and be unable to escape. It was too dark even to point, so he whispered right up against their ears, telling them where to set their claymores, reminding them where everyone else was, so they wouldn't go brain-dead and shoot at each other.

Happy thought.

One guy would dig a shallow, muddy trench — very, very quietly, while the other one pulled guard. Throughout the night, they would stand watch for an hour at a time, and then sleep for an hour. They would use the ponchos, mainly, for ground cover, since the rain made too much noise bouncing off them if they put them on.

Snoopy crept out to set out the claymore — the guy who didn't carry an entrenching tool carried a claymore, on this trip — and then came creeping back. Even though Michael knew he was coming, having a figure appear right on top of him still scared the hell out of him.

"First," Snoopy whispered.

"Okay," Michael whispered, and curled up in

the very small trench — how much protection would it really be? — to try and get some sleep.

He must have, because now Snoopy was waking him up, and they switched places without a word. It was drizzling, not as hard as before, but still mighty unpleasant. He had his towel over his head — but a hat would make life a lot easier. Relatively speaking.

It was wet, he was scared, and it was so dark that he couldn't even see the rest of his *squad*, let alone anything else.

It was going to be another long night.

CHAPTER 12

IT WAS 0340. It was very quiet. At least, as far as he could tell. Dark as it was, the whole NVA could walk by, and he probably wouldn't see a thing. But, he hadn't *heard* anything alarming. And, in twenty minutes, he could wake up Snoopy.

He checked his watch. Nineteen, now. Good. Except for the odd rustling or shifting, he couldn't really hear the others. Once, he heard Jankowski whisper into the radio, but that was all. He could start thinking nightmare thoughts — like that they were all gone, or someone had come and slit their throats, or something like that, but — hell with it. Better not to think at all.

He looked into the black and rain, and listened to mortars thump somewhere far away. It was scary out here, sure, but it was kind of — peace-

ful, too. He didn't mind it so much. It was almost — the mortars seemed closer, somehow,
but it was hard to tell. Hard for him, anyway.
But — they were definitely closer. There were a
lot of them. And they sounded different. They
sounded — they were hitting the NDP, that's
what they were doing. And if they weren't —
they were damned close. Oh, God.

Behind him, Snoopy woke up, and he could
hear everyone else moving around, too. Someone — it sounded like Sergeant Hanson — was
whispering into the radio, and a voice Michael
couldn't quite understand came crackling back.
But he could *definitely* hear mortars in the back-
ground. This couldn't be routine, it had to be
something — were they all right? Was the camp
being blown to bits? Were they next?

"Hold your positions," Sergeant Hanson said
quietly. "No matter what happens, we're here
'til first light."

There were answering mortars now, but no
gunfire that Michael could hear, so that probably
meant it was a probe, rather than a full-fledged
attack. Not that that meant people weren't getting maimed and killed. Like that poor son-of-
a-bitch, holding what was left of his arm today.
Oh, God.

The artillery went on and on, joined by the high-above whoosh of Phantom fighters, and their bombs crashing somewhere out in the jungle. Somewhere not too far away. He sure as hell hoped the pilots knew the grid coordinates of this ambush. And would avoid it. They were all on extra-alert, watching the empty trail, but it was hard to pay attention, wondering what was happening to everyone else. He didn't even know any of the guys in 2nd and 3rd Platoons, but — they were all in this together.

He heard helicopters at one point, which was worrisome, since it probably meant medevacs. Frustrating, not to know what was going on. Scary. Helpless.

Finally, just before 0500, all of the artillery and bombing stopped, leaving behind an eerie silence. The drizzle was still coming down, and all Michael could hear was that, and a vague ringing in his ears.

After a few minutes of the silence, he heard Jankowski whispering into the radio, a voice coming back, then more silence. What the hell was going on?

They waited. They watched. Nothing happened. Dawn was coming, and when it was just light enough to see each other, Sergeant Hanson motioned for J.D. and Finnegan to move out.

Michael looked at Snoopy, who whispered, "LP." Once they were out there, Sergeant Hanson motioned for one in each pair to go out, disconnect, and take in the claymores. Then, J.D. and Finnegan came back in, and they started back to the NDP, Sergeant Hanson taking point this time. Taking it slow. Taking a different route. Smart.

It was light out when they got back. There were a lot of craters in the jungle that hadn't been there the night before, but otherwise, things looked calm. They had stopped, right before pulling in, Jankowski calling in once again to be sure that everyone knew that they were coming, and exactly *where* they would be coming. No point taking chances.

Guys were up, and moving around, and making coffee and so forth. They looked maybe a little more tired and tense than usual, but otherwise, it seemed like the other mornings had seemed. Oddly casual. Oddly like the Boy Scouts.

"How bad was it?" J.D. asked, as they passed a guy shaving, using some water he'd poured into the bottom of his helmet.

"Y'all lucked out," the guy said, with a heavy Southern drawl. "Missed *all* the shit."

"Anyone hurt?" Finnegan asked.

The guy nodded, shaving away. "Couple guys, 3rd Platoon. Lee and McCarthy, I think. Then, Doc Mendez took some shrapnel, gittin' out there. Chopper dusted 'em off."

"They be all right?" Snoopy asked.

The guy shrugged. "Lee got fucked up bad. Y'all run into any a them?"

They shook their heads. The guy shook *his* head, and went back to shaving.

Doc Mendez. The medic in Three Squad. He actually kind of knew Doc Mendez. By sight, anyway. He'd gotten a malaria pill from him yesterday. Creepy. Awful.

"Word's we diggin' in today," the guy said after them. "So HQ gits a fix on them big old guns."

Michael looked at the others. Was this good news, or bad? Mixed, it would appear.

"Worms on a hook," Jankowski said, grimly, and the others nodded.

Sounded like they were going to spend the day — and night? — being bait. Oh, swell.

He nudged Snoopy. "We in trouble?"

Snoopy shrugged. "Won't be humping 'round the damn jungle, at least."

No, just being sitting ducks for mortars. Sounded like a mixed blessing.

The nearest crater to their particular foxhole was about fifty yards away. Kind of close for comfort. But, only a few seemed to have hit within the *actual* confines of the camp. So the enemy wasn't quite sure where they were. Yet.

Sergeant Hanson had disappeared to the CP, and when he came back, whistled the squad together.

"Okay," he said. "We're going to hold this position today. Dig in deep as you can, then grab some sleep. Three Squad's going to blow an LZ over there — " he pointed — "and we'll get re-supply this afternoon."

"*Yes*," Finnegan said.

"Today's a light one," Sergeant Hanson said, "but look alive. Don't know yet if we pull ambush tonight. We'll blow some timbers later, get fixed in for the night."

Everyone else looked pretty cheerful, so this must be good news.

"This is good?" he asked J.D., to be sure.

J.D. grinned at him. "It's a skate, man. It's *better* than a skate."

So, he and Snoopy dug for a while, fortifying

their sandbag walls, more than anything else. If they were going to blow timbers later, that meant, they would put them up on top, and pile sandbags on top of *that* to try and protect against mortars.

But, Snoopy was right — it was better than walking.

The hole was pretty deep now, and Snoopy curled up, down in the bottom. In the mud.

"Would you mind bringing me breakfast in bed, honey?" he asked, sweetly.

"Yes," Michael said, making some coffee.

"Even if I use the magic word?" Snoopy asked. Sweetly.

"Even if you use threats," Michael said. "Besides, we don't have a whole lot left *to* eat."

"Resupply, babe," Snoopy said, and put his helmet on over his head. Then, he took it off, and put it over his crotch instead.

"Not a whole lot to protect there," Michael said, opening some caraway cheese and crackers.

"More than *you* got," Snoopy said, and closed his eyes.

Michael was damned tired too, but he went out to check the claymores — in case some gook son-of-a-bitch had crawled in and flipped them around while they weren't here, or weren't looking. Gook. Damn. He was starting to use it, too. Then, he went to the bathroom, washed his face with some of the little remaining water he had left, and brushed his teeth with a tiny bit more. He spit a few times, trying to get the chalky taste out. He was mildly successful. The hygiene was only mildly successful, too.

On that note. He sat down on some sandbags, looked around to make sure things seemed pretty secure, then unlaced his boots. He had changed his socks a couple of times — in the last few days — and, without much optimism, sprinkled on some foot powder, but they felt clammy and unpleasant all the time, anyway. If today was a skate, he might as well take advantage of it, and give his feet a little air, maybe. A little change of scene.

They were disgusting. They smelled. *He* smelled. If Elizabeth thought he was a bum before, she would *really* hate him now.

Oh, come on. She *already* hated him.

Hell with it.

He washed his feet with what was left in his canteen, then dried them with his towel. Yes, the same towel he'd be wearing around his neck, or over his head, later today.

FTA, man. FTA.

Fuck everything.

Like UC/Boulder was the be-all and end-all, anyway. Like she knew everything. Like he even gave a damn.

He looked at his feet. They looked awful. Not like the feet he remembered belonging to him for the last eighteen years. Not that he was a walk-around-barefoot-marveling-at-the-beauty-of-the-day kind of guy, but — he knew what his feet were supposed to look like. *Not* ghost-white, wrinkled, and bubbling with blisters. Disgusting.

Hey, if she saw him with these feet, he wouldn't even *mind* if she blew him off. Well — it'd make sense, at least. More sense.

Things were quiet, so he decided to leave his boots off for a while, let them dry out a little.

Doc Adams came over with malaria pills.

"Good," he said, his expression approving. "Your feets, your best friend here."

"They're kind of messed-up," Michael said. Kind of?

Doc bent to examine them, then straightened up. "Kid, hate to tell you, you got 'bout the best-lookin' feet in the company."

In that case, he didn't even want to think about what boots around him hid. "Is there anything I can do?" he asked.

"Not really. They get worse, I give you some salve, but . . ." Doc shrugged. "Keep 'em dry, best you can."

Michael nodded, and swallowed his malaria pill. Dry.

Doc looked approving, making a little check mark on a piece of paper. Company list, looked like. "How you doin' for salt, kid?" he asked.

Kid. "Little low," Michael said.

Doc nodded, gave him some more, then grinned. "Not gonna cuss me out for callin' you kid?"

"I'll cut you some slack," Michael said, and paused. "This time."

"Oooh. Guess I been *warned*." Doc patted his head, then crouched by the foxhole. "Snoopers, wake up, kid."

Snoopy looked up, bleary-eyed.

"Just pop it, kid, then go back to sleep," Doc said.

Snoopy obediently gulped the pill down, then went right back to sleep without missing a beat.

"The kid amazes me," Doc said, getting up. "Which ain't easy."

Considering that he'd slept through Three Squad blowing the LZ, it *was* amazing.

"Uh, Doc?" Michael said, as he headed for

J.D. and Finnegan's hole. "The guys? From last night?"

Doc's smile faded. "Lee got it bad." He shook his head. "Real bad."

Oh. He didn't know Lee. Didn't have to.

When his feet felt dry — drier — he put his boots back on. The foxhole was pretty small, and he didn't want to disturb Snoopy, so he folded his flak jacket, put his head down, and stretched out next to the sandbags. That'd give him a *little* protection, at least. Anyway, the saying was, GIs own the day, VC own the night.

Besides. He was really tired.

He woke up in the late morning, because it was so damned hot. Too damned hot. Which made him think of his mother, and the musicals she always played on their old record player. Loudly. Always made him laugh. Not much of a singer, his mother.

"The princess!" Finnegan chirped, slouched against his sandbags a few meters away, cleaning his gun. "She awakes!"

Michael grinned. "You're a jerk, Finnegan."

"You, too, Meat," Finnegan said, and squirted a little LSA at him. Lubricant, Small Arms.

Hell, it smelled better than *he* did.

He sat up, more awake now. Christ, it was hot. Most of the guys had their shirts off, and he took his off, too. Hey, might as well get as much sunburn as possible.

"Snoopy still crashed out?" Finnegan asked, squirting some more LSA.

Michael looked into the foxhole. "Yup."

"Saw him fall asleep right in the middle of a C-rat once," Finnegan said. "I mean, right *in* it."

Easy to picture. Michael leaned up against his own sandbags. "Think we'll get hit again tonight?"

Finnegan nodded, cleaning his gun.

Oh.

CHAPTER 13

NO REASON to let that ruin his day. He guessed. He leaned against the sandbags, looking up at the sky. He needed some shades. He needed a boonie hat. He needed some iced tea. Or lemonade. Lemonade would be great.

"What were you doing?" Finnegan asked. "When they got you."

Michael opened his eyes. "Skiing."

"Meant for a job," Finnegan said. "Or, you just graduate?"

"That was my job," Michael said.

"For real?"

Michael nodded. "My father has a gas station, and I helped him out some, too."

"You know cars?" Finnegan asked.

He pronounced "cars" with an "h," not an "r." Sounded like a damned Kennedy. "I'm okay," Michael said.

"You got experience," Finnegan said, "and they didn't give you motor pool?" Motah pool.

"Of course not," Michael said. "That would make too much sense."

Finnegan nodded, and cleaned his gun.

"What were you doing?" Michael asked.

Finnegan grinned wryly. "Stupid enough to beat them to it."

"You *volunteered*?" Michael said.

Finnegan nodded, wryly. A leprechaun who no longer felt so sly. "Figured sooner I got it out of the way, sooner I could join the cops."

"I never volunteer," Michael said. "It's one of my rules."

"One of mine now, too," Finnegan said. "Except for spelling J.D. at point."

A football came flying in-between them.

"Hey, watch it, Thumper!" Finnegan said, and threw it back. Pretty good spiral.

Michael turned to see Thumper playing catch with Bear. Red-blooded American boys, in the middle of a war zone. "He humps that?" he asked.

Finnegan nodded. "Doesn't want to lose his touch."

In that case, maybe he should be carrying his skis around. Waxing them every time they took a break, and all. "Isn't anyone keeping watch?" he asked.

"Yeah." Finnegan started reassembling his gun. "L-T sent some patrols out."

Well — okay. "Do you really carry a Ted Williams ball?" he asked.

Finnegan grinned. "Weapon of last resort."

Michael grinned, too. "What if they didn't throw it back?"

"I wouldn't be happy," Finnegan said. From the sound of his voice, an extreme understatement. The M-16 was reassembled, and he started cleaning his ammunition.

Michael watched him. "Do we really need to do that?"

Finnegan nodded. "Gets wet, gets muddy." Then, he shrugged. "Can't hurt."

Okay. Michael reached for a magazine, and started popping the bullets out. Anyway, it gave him something to do.

Viper walked by, yawning, a cigarette in one corner of his mouth.

"How you doin', Viper?" Finnegan asked.

Viper nodded, exhaled some smoke in a friendly way, and continued ambling along.

"Doesn't talk much, does he," Michael said.

"You should have seen this Indian guy we had," Finnegan said. "Think he was Cherokee, or something. Don't think I ever *heard* his voice. Best damn shot I ever saw, though."

"He, uh, isn't here anymore?" Michael asked, knowing that he should probably just keep his mouth shut.

"Ran out of luck," Finnegan said stiffly.

Oh.

"My ball," Finnegan said, recovering, "it's lucky. I don't even go take a piss without my ball." He pulled it out of his pocket, to demonstrate that he, indeed, always had it.

"Can you see the bat mark?" Michael asked.

Finnegan nodded, flipping it over to him. Michael caught it automatically, and looked at the smudge. Ted Williams. Okay, he was kind of impressed. Just for fun, he drew his arm back, and pretended he was about to throw it out into the jungle.

"Hey!" Finnegan protested, about to lunge for him.

Michael grinned, and flipped it back.

"You think it's funny?" Finnegan examined the ball for possible minute damage. "It's not funny."

"It's kind of funny," Michael said.

"*Ted Williams,*" Finnegan said. "You got no respect."

Michael grinned, cleaning his bullets.

J.D.'s head popped out of his foxhole. "Got any more paper, you sonovabitch?" he asked Finnegan.

"So you can write to *her* again?" Finnegan asked.

J.D. nodded.

"Boring," Finnegan said. "Check my ruck, you sonovabitch. And get my radio, will ya? We need tunes."

"Is it really — safe?" Michael asked, as Finnegan turned it on. "Listening out here?"

Finnegan shrugged. "Sarge yells at me, I turn it off. He doesn't, I keep it on."

Hmmm.

Otis Redding, and "Sitting on the Dock of the Bay" was just starting. Snoopy woke up instantly.

"Hey, I love that song," he said, climbing out of the foxhole. "Turn it up."

Finnegan looked around for Sergeant Hanson, then turned it up.

"What if someone — shoots at us?" Michael asked.

Finnegan shrugged. "Even Victor Charlie likes tunes."

Snoopy shrugged, too. "They shoot us, shortens up our tours some."

Happy thought.

J.D.'s head popped up, suddenly. "If they were only going on a three-hour tour, how come Ginger and Mrs. Howell brought so many clothes?"

They all looked at him.

"Don't know, man," Finnegan said.

"It bothers me," J.D. said, and disappeared back into the foxhole.

Sergeant Hanson came over. "That's too loud, Finnegan."

Finnegan turned it down. A little.

"Better, but still not great." He looked at Michael and Snoopy. "You two looking for something to do?"

No.

"Clear out more of that brush." He pointed in front of their position. "Your field of fire sucks."

They nodded.

"*Now,* would be good," he said.

They got up.

"Do *not* trip your claymores," he said.

Good idea.

J.D.'s head popped up. "Why did Ginger and Mrs. Howell bring so many clothes, Sarge? And supplies and all?"

Sergeant Hanson thought about that. "Women," he said finally. "Women are very practical." He looked at Michael and Snoopy. "I don't see you moving. I see you still standing here."

They moved.

At about 1500, everyone who had gone out on night ambush went out to the jungle with machetes and what little C-4 they had left to blow timber. Blow up trees, in other words. A little reconnaissance patrol went first, to check for mines, and for possible ambushes. They didn't find anything, so everyone went out, and got to work, chopping the trees down and dragging the logs back to the perimeter.

It was hot, and heavy, work, but Michael had spent enough time over the years chopping wood with his father that it felt familiar enough not to bother him much. Some guy in 2nd Platoon, who grew up in the mountains of West Virginia and had one of the strongest — and strangest — accents he'd ever heard, told him that it was the city boys, couldn't never drag theirselfs no lumber. That they was plumb useless.

Considering that Snoopy — the kid from Newark — and some guy with a heavy Brooklyn accent were complaining more than anyone else, maybe this was true. Mostly everyone was complaining a little, but in a pretty benign way. "What are we, fucking forest rangers?" seemed to be the general attitude. Then, some dumb redneck suggested that Snoopy and some of the other guys looked more like jungle bunnies, and things got a little ugly — melting pot versus rednecks — before Sergeant Hanson, swearing and scowling, broke it up. There were some words, and some shoving, but no punches. The redneck looked quelled — but not enough, insisting that he'd just been, Christ the Lord, kidding. It was suggested that he'd better shape up. Effective immediately.

Michael was working with Jankowski and Viper — who didn't get into the fight, but looked dangerous as hell, either way.

"New guys," he growled. "Don't know how to act."

"Me too?" Michael couldn't resist asking.

Viper looked at him, briefly. "Don't know

'bout you yet," he said, and went back to chopping.

Oh. Well, okay. He had a little honest and direct streak of his own. Michael went back to chopping, too.

Sergeant Hanson came over, still visibly angry, taking Jankowski's machete and giving the nearest tree a couple of good hard whacks before handing it back.

"Least he ain't in *our* platoon," Jankowski said.

Sergeant Hanson nodded, exchanged glances with Viper, then went back to supervise the others.

It took quite a while to drag the logs back, and they piled a couple on top of each foxhole, then started the work of filling sandbags to add even more protection above. It was a lot of work, building bunkers they were just going to take apart the next day, but — like Snoopy said — it was better than humping around the jungle.

At a little past 1700, resupply came in, and all work was instantly suspended, everyone grabbing whatever letters they had written, to be taken back to base camp and mailed. J.D. had the most, seemed like, but Michael was surprised to see Viper with a small stack, too. Still waters.

The resupply was lots of C-rats and ammo, five-gallon jerry cans of fresh water — *Yes,* Finnegan said — hot food, some oranges — oh, *yes,* Finnegan said — cigarettes, soda and beer, new socks, and mail. Again, everyone went for the mail first.

Michael wasn't figuring on getting any, so he helped the three new guys who had also come in on the chopper, and were being completely ignored. Felt familiar. They looked scared, too. He kind of hoped he had looked a little more cool than that. He also kind of doubted it.

"You been out here forever?" one of them asked him.

Hot damn, they thought he was a veteran. Well, hell, he *was* getting some salt stains on his boots and all. "Only feels like forever," he said, unloading the last of the crates, and the chopper took off.

"Yo, Jennings!" He heard the sergeant from 3rd Platoon saying, as he handed out the mail. "Anyone know Jennings?"

Mail? Wow. Michael went over to collect the letter, recognizing his mother's handwriting. He carried it over to his foxhole to read. Everyone in the squad had at least one, so morale was in pretty good shape.

"My grandmother wants to be sure I'm keeping warm enough," Snoopy said, reading.

It was at least ninety-five degrees — probably more, and even with their shirts off, they were all sweating like pigs.

"Maybe she'll send you a sweater," Michael said, making himself comfortable against the side of the bunker.

Snoopy nodded. "Says right here, she'll knit me up one, if I want. If I'm allowed to wear it with my uniform."

"Get the boy a cardigan," Finnegan said, reading.

"And then get him an Article 15," J.D. said, looking at a couple of photographs. Emily, probably.

Michael took his time opening his letter, wanting to savor it. Looking at his mother's handwriting — which he'd seen on a hell of a lot of grocery lists over the years — made him very homesick. Made his throat hurt again.

Sergeant Hanson came over with enough beer for everyone, and a letter of his own, which he plopped down to read. He looked pleased, so it was probably from a girl, too.

Michael, savoring away, took his time, opening his beer first and drinking some. Nice and cold. Tasted great. Now, he took the letter out.

> Dear Mike,
>
> We haven't heard from you yet, so I sure hope everything's all right. We know what a hard time you must be having, and I can't help worrying. Your father and I look at the news every night, hoping we'll see right where you are. The President keeps talking about peace, and I sure hope he means it. You only just got over there, but every day, I pray for when you'll come back to us.
>
> I hope you're making friends — I know how shy you are. I hope the other boys are nice, and you have someone you can talk to. Otis sure misses you. He's just fine, and eating as much as ever, but he's mopey. I keep telling Dennis and Carrie to give him some extra attention, until you get back. I guess your father thinks it's silly, but I'm already counting the days.

It wasn't all that silly. Everyone over *here* was counting the days.

All these rumors and peace talks — I just pray they're true. Poor LBJ looks so sad, but I can't help blaming him. You know how much your father and I dislike Mr. Goldwater, but if he would have done something to bring you boys home . . . or never let you go.

I wasn't sure if I should tell you this, but I ran into Lizzy the other day at the market. She sure was surprised to hear that you had gone, and she wanted your address. I thought I'd better check with you first, after the hard time you had.

Michael lowered the letter. Oh, *great.* Like he didn't have enough problems, without her writing him. It was too late for a Dear John letter, but that didn't mean she would find nice things to say. Lecture him about UC/Boulder, probably. About how smart she was now.

Hell with it. He went back to the letter.

Your father says to tell you Mr. Wright brought in that old Impala again. A cracked engine block, this time, but he still won't give it up. He sure does miss you. Your father, I mean. Although maybe Mr. Wright

does, too, all the time you've spent to-
gether(!) We all miss you. Please write,
dear, and let me know that you're okay.

Love, Mom

Then, at the bottom,

Hi, Mikey! What's it like over there? It
sure looks scary from here. Mom keeps say-
ing she's afraid you won't eat enough, and
she hated how skinny you were when you
were here on leave. I got all A's again, and
Dad took us out to dinner, and said we
could get anything we wanted. Dennis only
got one C, so Mom and Dad weren't mad
at him. Didn't seem right without you there,
and Mom was all teary. I was pretty em-
barrassed. Don't let Lizzy write to you —
I think she's mean. I was teaching Otis a
new trick, but he forgot it. Beatles, 4-ever!

Love and Xs, Carrie

Yeah, she was still dotting her i's with little
flowers. Fourteen years old, and still mad that
she hadn't been able to participate in the Summer
of Love. Talked about Haight-Ashbury — not

that she'd ever been to California — like it was their own backyard. Cute kid, his sister.

Michael read through the letter a couple more times, then very carefully folded it, and put it in his pocket. Like hell he'd burn it so the enemy wouldn't get ahold of it. The enemy was going to have to get ahold of *him* first.

"Mom and Dad?" Snoopy asked.

Michael nodded, and drank some beer. Mom, anyway. Dad, in spirit, he guessed. His father wasn't much of a talking guy, but Michael usually pretty much knew where he stood with him. Anyway, Dennis was the one who always got in trouble. Always goofed off. Michael was the serious one. The quiet one. Yeah, the one they worried about. They thought he was too sensitive. No way, not *this* GI.

Everyone else was still reading and rereading, except for Jankowski, who was crowing over the little box of spices and seasonings his mother had sent him. Anything, *anything*, to perk up C-rats. Maybe he should have asked his mother for stuff like that too, instead of just the Kool-Aid.

J.D. laughed, reading over Finnegan's shoulder. "Father McDougal misses you singing at Mass? Oh, you lame sonova bitch."

"You sing at church?" Michael said, also laughing. And probably *did* pass the collection plate.

"Yeah," Finnegan said, then added to the group in general, "got a problem with that?"

No one had a problem with it. But, everyone thought it was funny.

Snoopy smacked Michael across the back of the head. "Come on," he said. "I'm 'bout as hungry as a young man can be."

Michael nodded, getting up, feeling soggy from the heat. Truth was, he was pretty hungry, too. And, he was guessing, there was an orange over there with his name on it.

One of the new guys was in front of them in line, and obviously self-conscious, he helped himself tentatively to some of the spaghetti and meatballs, spilling a good-sized spoonful in the dirt. Big meatballs. Beef, Michael hoped. With the Army, you could never quite be sure.

"Pitiful," Snoopy said.

Michael grinned. Only a few days out here, and he was already part of the boonierat ritual. Talk about survival of the fittest. "Just as pitiful as can be," he said.

CHAPTER 14

HE AND SNOOPY only had to pull perimeter that night, but the mortars started coming in around 0300. And coming, and coming, and coming. All they could do, was scrunch down real low, helmet and flak jacket as tight as can be, and just hope not to take a direct hit. He thought he heard a couple of screams out there somewhere, but they might have just been fear screams, not pain screams. He hoped. He kind of felt like screaming himself. He felt *just* like screaming.

He couldn't tell how close the shells were landing — most of them seemed to be outside the perimeter, but at one point, shrapnel thudded against their sandbags. Maybe a lot of pieces, maybe just a couple. He was already as low as he could go, but he tried to make himself even smaller than that. Impossibly small. He could feel the ground shaking, he could feel Snoopy shaking, he could feel *himself* shaking.

It was unbelievably loud already, but the addition of American firepower was deafening. F-4s thundering above, sending full payloads of bombs and napalm down into the night; FSB Joanne sending their own artillery out. It went on and on, and they must have knocked out the NVA guns, because the incoming stopped. Now, gunships were out strafing the jungle, and Michael poked his head up just enough to look out and check the perimeter. He couldn't see anything, but then, someone somewhere in the camp sent a flare up, and in the arcing glow, he was able to see that the area was clear. That they weren't storming in.

"Willie McCovey," a voice said quietly behind them.

Tonight's signal. Sergeant Hanson slid into their foxhole.

"You two okay?" he asked.

"Yeah," Michael said, his voice coming out high.

"Unh-hunh," Snoopy said, not sounding too steady himself.

"Okay. I think it's over for tonight, but keep

a sharp eye." He slid out of the hole. "We're pulling out, 0600."

"Is anyone hit?" Snoopy asked.

"Doesn't look that way. Their aim wasn't too good tonight. Look alive, in case they assault," he said, and then crawled to the next hole.

Assault? Michael's heart felt as if it were thumping all over his chest, as if the bombs were still landing somewhere inside him.

"That was — that was something," he said weakly, trying to get his breath.

Snoopy reached outside with one nervous hand, feeling the sandbags. "Damn near bought it," he whispered. "This one's fuckin' shredded."

Jesus. Worms on a hook. They were nothing more than worms on a hook. Jesus Christ Almighty. He propped his M-16 up on the sandbags, feeling the shredding for himself, his hands beginning to shake even more.

0410. That was *all*? It had seemed like centuries.

Platoon sweeps, again. 3rd Platoon would be staying behind a couple of hours, to police the area, and load unused equipment and empty resupply containers onto a soon-to-arrive chopper, while the other two platoons moved out. It was almost going to be a relief to get back out into the jungle and, at least, be a *moving* target. Sitting, and waiting, was much, much worse.

2nd Platoon was never going to be more than about a klick away from them today, and they were both going to sweep down the hill, and across a sort of valley to some more hills. 3rd Platoon would sweep straight ahead, instead of curving out, so they would be able to catch up. Michael sure hoped there was a point to all of this. Some sort of higher logic.

No one seemed to be very hungry, and when the call came to "saddle up!", they were ready quickly. Lieutenant Brady told them Intelligence had it that a company of main-force VC had fled the hills, and gone down into the valley. So, they were going after them.

Better to pursue than be pursued. Right?

1st Squad had had a slack day the day before, so they were on point. Meaning poor old J.D. was on point. They moved out, down the hill, through thick underbrush, everyone sweaty and out of breath before they'd even gone one hundred meters. They stumbled along endlessly, Michael walking fifth today, behind Viper. He and Snoopy were each carrying some of the M-60 ammunition, in addition to all their regular stuff. But Viper had the bulk of it, and with all that weight, he still walked steadily along, never seeming to sag or falter. Michael sagged and faltered repeatedly.

They stopped to rest, finally, and Lieutenant Brady decided to have them change directions and veer back onto the trail so they could make up some time. While they were waiting, Michael managed to choke down some water and a can of warm fruit cocktail, and then they were on their way again.

The sun was high in the sky, and it was getting very goddamn hot.

There was a stream somewhere up ahead — Michael could hear it, and he was already looking forward to the idea that he would maybe be able to top off one or two of his canteens as they passed through it. Pour some over his head, too. Try to cool down. But they were barely within sight of it, still on the riverbank, when J.D. dropped down, raising one arm in the stop signal, then wiggling three fingers, everyone else dropping, and passing the signs back.

Three wiggling fingers meant three enemy soldiers. Meant that he actually *saw* them. Oh, Christ. Michael had to gulp a couple of times, his hand ready to flip the selector switch and get his gun off safety. His hand was a lot more ready than the rest of him.

Sergeant Hanson went hustling silently up to the front, then hustled back, motioning for Two Squad to move out in a flanking motion on this side of the stream. He passed some signals to Lieutenant Brady, who began leading Three Squad around the other way.

Michael wasn't sure who fired first, but suddenly, there seemed to be bullets coming from everywhere — and he hadn't even seen anyone yet. He flattened to the ground, remembering to flip the gun to semi, instead of full automatic, and then squeezed off several shots in what he hoped was the right direction.

"Guns up!" Sergeant Hanson yelled, and Viper was already on the run, then throwing himself down, shoving the M-60 into position. Snoopy went diving next to him, so he could feed the gun, and Viper began laying down serious fire, all across the stream.

"Covering fire!" Sergeant Hanson yelled.

Michael was trying to figure out if he should crawl up there, too, or throw one of his frags, or what, when he heard a whistling, and the dust kicked up in front of him. Bullets! *Christ!* He rolled hard to his right, but came up firing, mad

as hell that someone was shooting at him. At
him, in particular. Like they knew him personally, or something.

More dust. Jesus! He rolled behind a rock,
about the size of a basketball, trying to keep his
head down. He caught sight of a muzzle flash,
across the stream, and grabbed one of his frags,
armed it, then threw it as hard as he could out
where he had seen the flash. Then, he ducked
down, bullets skipping in the water out in front
of him.

The grenade exploded — but he couldn't tell
if it had any effect or not. And they were still
firing. Now what?

He had run through a full magazine now, and
he yanked it out, turning it around and snapping
another in. J.D. had told him he should tape
magazines together, back to back, to save time
in a firefight, and now he was damned glad he
had done it.

Except — he was scared. For a moment, he
was so scared he couldn't move, frozen there on
his side, trying to gulp in something other than
smoke and the smell of gunpowder. He huddled
there, too scared to move, but then realized
someone might see him, and so lifted himself up

enough to fire off a few more, trying to shoot where everyone else was shooting.

"Hold your fire!" Sergeant Hanson was yelling. "Hold your fucking fire!"

The shooting died down, then ceased, and the smell of cordite hung thick in the air. There was a long silence, then a voice — L-T? — yelling, "Thumper! Smitty! Move up!"

More silence.

"All clear, One-Six!" a voice yelled.

"We got *two* a' the suckers!" another voice chimed in.

There was a fair amount of elation over this, although Michael felt more sick than anything else. Lieutenant Brady assigned a couple of guys to strip the bodies of maps and other possible intelligence, then sent a few more to see if they could pick up any blood trails, which they couldn't. So, the final verdict — tally — score — was two confirmed enemy KIA, size of force unknown. HQ would be pleased.

What was even more amazing, with all that shooting, was that *they* hadn't sustained any serious casualties at all. A kid in Three Squad had his arm creased by a bullet, and barely needed a band-aid, and Washington, in Two Squad, had given his ankle a wrench. Neither needed an evac.

After talking to the company CO, Lieutenant Brady gave the word that they were going to pull back a little, and wait for 2nd Platoon to link up with them, so they could pursue the VC's probable line of flight.

Everyone was still pretty charged up, as they moved to a clearing off the trail, Lieutenant Brady immediately on the horn to pass the appropriate coordinates to the 2nd Platoon leader. "Confirmed, man," everyone was saying, "when's the last time we had actual *confirmed*?" Everyone was hyper and cheerful and cracking open C-rats — it'd be a good twenty, at least, until 2nd Platoon could get to them.

Finnegan took out his Ted Williams ball and kissed it. "Kiss it for luck, man," he said, flipping it to J.D. "Better than the Blarney Stone."

"All I want to kiss is this canteen," J.D. said, but he caught the ball, anyway, and flipped it up in the air.

Michael took his helmet off and put it on the ground, then sat down on it. Confirmed kills. Christ. He took out a cigarette, hoping that smoking it would steady his nerves some. He wasn't cut out for this. He wasn't tough enough.

A guy he didn't really know grinned at him, seeing the cigarette. "Good as sex, hunh?" he said.

Sick. Kind of funny, but sick. "Nothing's as good as sex," Michael said, and lit up.

Snoopy sat down next to him. "Was that you, hucking grenades, like you actually knew what the hell you were doing?"

"Can't think who that was," Michael said, and released some smoke. It helped. A little.

"I gotta find some shade," J.D. said, looking around, flipping the ball idly with one hand. "I'm *way* too short for this shit." He headed for a nearby tree. "I'm so short I — "

The sound of the explosion sent everyone diving to the ground, looking for cover. And, at first, when — stuff — rained down, Michael wasn't sure what it was. Then, he realized *who* it was. Who it had been. That one second, J.D. had been walking around, alive and whole, and just looking to get out of the sun; and the next second, he was — there was nothing left but — it must have been some kind of mine, or — and now J.D. was —

Oh, Jesus.

Oh, no.

Oh, God.

At first, it was absolutely silent; then, the only sound was Snoopy throwing up. Nobody said anything; nobody moved. Nobody could quite take in what had just happened. Finnegan, who had been the closest to him — yeah, more ways than one — didn't seem to be hurt, but he was covered with — stuff. With what was left of his best friend. And now he was just standing there, too dazed to move, covered with — blood that wasn't his.

Someone had to do something. Someone had to do something *fast*.

Nobody was doing anything.

Michael yanked the towel from around his neck, spilled canteen water onto it, then moved swiftly over next to Finnegan, bending to wash the blood and gore off his face. Out of his hair, from his neck and shoulders, spilling precious water over him to wash — everything — away. To get all of it *off* him. Quickly.

"It's okay, you're okay, man," he heard himself saying, over and over again. "You're going to be okay."

Finnegan's shirt was beyond saving — beyond imagination, really — and Michael pulled his knife out, cutting it off him and tossing it aside.

"Sorry, man," he said, calmly — Jesus, hadn't anyone else moved yet? Were they going to? — "Tore your shirt. Here, take mine." He had his own shirt off now, pulling it onto Finnegan, who still didn't seem to realize what was happening. What had already happened.

Michael sponged off his face again, then his pants and boots, doing the best he could to get rid of — everything.

Oh, God. Oh, Christ.

"Is it all off me?" Finnegan whispered, in a tiny little voice.

It. He.

"It's okay," Michael said. "You're going to be okay." He stood up, the rest of the platoon — even Sergeant Hanson; almost especially, Sergeant Hanson — still completely, silently stunned. Staring at him. Not moving. "The man needs a drink," he said. Almost barked. "Someone get over here with a drink!"

Jankowski reacted first, pulling a flask out of his rucksack and bringing it over, Doc right behind him. Now, the only sound was Jankowski saying, "come on, man, have some of this, it's good for you, come on." Other than that, it was still silent, nobody able to look at anyone — or anything — else.

"*Lieutenant,*" Michael said. Ordered, actually.

Lieutenant Brady snapped out of it. "I, uh — I — " He fumbled inside his rucksack, taking out a body bag. "Men — " He looked sick. "Men, I need a volunteer."

If possible, it got even quieter.

Oh, shit. "Right," Michael said, and stepped forward to take the bag. He looked at Sergeant Hanson. "We're going to need an LZ, Sarge." Assuming that Sergeant Hanson would take it from there, he went back over to Finnegan.

"Is Jimmy okay?" Finnegan asked, his voice very small.

Oh, Christ. Jimmy. Who even knew his name was anything but J.D.? Michael bent down. "He didn't feel a thing," he said quietly. "Didn't even have time to be scared."

Finnegan stared at him, dazed.

"You were lucky to have known him," Michael said. "You go on over there with these guys, okay?" He pointed.

Finnegan nodded, slowly standing up, Jankowski and Doc on either side of him, taking him away.

Now, he was alone. He was alone, and he had to clean up the most awful thing in the world.

More awful than anything he could ever have imagined.

And something he was pretty sure he couldn't do.

"Let's just start," a voice behind him said.

Michael turned. Viper. "They need your help with the LZ," he said.

"*You* need my help," Viper said.

Michael nodded.

"Put your flak on," Viper said. "Let's take it slow."

Michael nodded.

At first, they worked in absolute silence. There wasn't much to find, and what there was, was awful. Viper moved first, checking for more booby traps, and then, together, they would pick up what they could.

This wasn't real. This couldn't possibly be real.

Behind them, he could hear Lieutenant Brady on the radio, calling for a dust-off. Reporting a Kilo-India-Alpha.

Jesus. J.D. Poor Emily. He didn't even *know* Emily. He'd only known J.D. a few days. Seemed much longer.

"Take yo'self a lesson," Viper said softly.

Michael looked up from the ground.

"Make yo'self some nice acquaintances, fine,"
Viper said. "But *never* make yo'self a friend you
can't stand to lose." He looked back in the direction Finnegan had gone. Had been taken.
"We'll watch him, but that poor son-of-a-bitch'll
be lucky to last a week. Always happens that
way."

Jesus. Michael swallowed.

"Meat." Now, Viper spoke even more softly.
"Snoopy's real careless, *real* often."

Michael stared at him.

"You know what I'm saying to you?" Viper
asked.

Yes. Didn't *want* to know it. Michael couldn't
look at him.

"You can watch him real close, like Sarge and
me, but it's something you best think about,"
Viper said.

"Jesus," Michael said. Quietly.

Off the radio now, Lieutenant Brady came
over to help them finish, all three of them struggling not to get sick. And maybe the worst
thing — no, it wasn't the worst, by a long shot —
was that they found the ball. It still looked pretty
much the same. Still had the bat mark. It didn't
seem right to leave it there, it didn't seem right
to throw it in the body bag, so Michael put it

carefully at the bottom of his ruck. Where Finnegan would be sure not to see it. Where he wouldn't have to see it, either.

"Better get 'em out of here quick, L-T," Viper said, softly. "They're gonna be real hinky."

Lieutenant Brady nodded, and slowly zipped up the body bag. Then, he looked at the two of them. "Pretend it's heavier than it is," he said.

Pretend they found more than they did. Michael and Viper nodded, each taking an end — as though it were — full — while Lieutenant Brady carried their gear.

"Meat," Viper said.

Michael looked up.

"Think I made up my mind 'bout you," he said.

Michael smiled, weakly; Viper gave him something a little bit like a smile back; and they carried the body bag to the LZ. They could already hear the medevac approaching.

"I can take it from here, kid," Sergeant Hanson said.

Michael nodded gratefully.

Sergeant Hanson took his end of the bag, looked startled for a second, then also pretended that it was heavy.

Michael's legs felt so shaky he wasn't sure he

could stay on his feet, but he did, opening his last full canteen, and washing his face. A couple of times. He felt a hand on his back, and looked over to see Snoopy standing next to him. Snoopy. He was *already* too close to Snoopy.

"Take a load off, man," Snoopy said.

Michael shook his head. If he sat down, he was afraid he wasn't going to be able to get himself to get up. To push on. To in any way keep fighting this war. This nightmare. He saw Finnegan, standing next to Doc, looking both stricken and angry, nodding his head over and over as Doc talked to him.

"Is he staying?" Michael asked.

Snoopy nodded. "Says he wants to."

Oh, God. Michael felt like crying. Not that he would be the only one.

"So, this guy," Snoopy said now, talking to everyone in general, giving Michael a little smack. "He's a cherry, right? Pushiest bastard you ever did see. As you all know, I had to beat the hell out of him, couple times already. And — I think I'm going to have to do it regular. I think he's trouble, that's what I think. But, luckily, old Snoopy here, is on the job. Everything'll be just fine."

No one was actually smiling — God knows — but some of the tension went out of the air.

"On the other hand," Snoopy said, "he just *loves* ham and limas, and if any of y'all want to trade, he always will."

"I *never* will," Michael said, his voice feeling strange inside his mouth. Unfamiliar.

"Well, then, you are looking for many more smacks," Snoopy said.

The tension eased. It had to. No matter who it was, no matter how it had happened, they were still out here. Still had to keep it together. *Had* to.

The chopper came, and went. Was gone.

It was quiet.

"Okay." Sergeant Hanson broke the silence, taking charge. Thank God. "We've got 2nd Platoon holding about three hundred meters away — we've got a ways to go yet. Let's saddle up!"

They did.

GLOSSARY

AIT: Advanced Infantry (or Individual) Training

AK-47: Russian-made automatic assault rifle, used by NVA and VC troops

AO: Area of Operations

ARVN: Army of the Republic of Vietnam (South Vietnam)

Article 15: disciplinary action taken against a soldier, usually because of insubordination; much less serious than a court martial

B-rations: reconstituted food rations

Boonie hat: soft-brimmed hat

Boonierat: slang for infantry soldier

Boonies: slang for being out in the field

The bush: slang for being out in the field

C-4: plastic explosive

Charlie: slang for Viet Cong

Cherry: slang for new, inexperienced soldier

Chop-chop: slang for food

Claymore mine: antipersonnel mine (US-made; hundreds of tiny steel balls propelled forward by a charge of plastic explosive upon detonation)

CP: Command Post

C-rations: canned combat rations, eaten in the field

DEROS: Date of Estimated Return from Overseas

Deuce-and-a-half: two-and-a-half-ton truck; used for transport

Didi: Vietnamese for "go quickly" or run

Dink: derogatory slang referring to Viet Cong; often referred to *any* Vietnamese person

Dinky-dau: Americanized version of Vietnamese expression for "crazy"

DMZ: Demilitarized Zone; a narrow strip of land dividing North Vietnam from South Vietnam

Door-gunner: soldier who sits in the bay of a helicopter, firing his gun in an attempt to protect the helicopter and crew

Dust-off: emergency medical evacuation by helicopter; also, the helicopter itself

Eleven-Bravo: MOS for an infantryman

EM Club: Enlisted Men's Club

Entrenching tool: small, collapsible shovel

EOD: Explosive Ordnance Disposal

Firebase: (also *FSB, Fire Support Base*) an artillery battery set up to provide fire support to units out in the field. Sometimes, firebases are permanent; other times, they exist only temporarily, before being torn down and relocated.

Frag grenade: fragmentation hand grenade, carried by soldiers

GI: slang for soldier; officially — government issue

Gook: derogatory slang for the Viet Cong and NVA; often, used for all Vietnamese

Grunt: slang for infantryman, or boonierat

Gunship: combat attack helicopter; will assault suspected or confirmed enemy positions to assist soldiers in the field

Heat tabs: inflammable tablets, provided to heat C-rations in the field; not always effective

H & I: Harassment and Interdiction fire; harassing barrage of artillery fire sent in direction of suspected enemy locations

Hootch: bunker or tent, used as shelter for military personnel; also, used to describe dwelling where villagers live

HQ: headquarters

Hump: carrying a heavy load while marching on patrol

I Corps: the northernmost military region of South Vietnam

K-bar: military knife

KIA: Killed in Action; sometimes, stated by military code — Kilo-India-Alpha

Klick: kilometer

KP: Kitchen Police; a work detail in the kitchen; generally given as punishment for minor infractions

LAW: Light Antitank Weapon; also, known as M-72

LBJ: Long Binh Jail (the stockade for military personnel in Vietnam)

Lifer: derogatory reference to career soldiers

LP: Listening Post

LRRP: Long Range Reconnaissance Patrol; also, refers to the members of said patrol; pronounced "Lurp"

LSA: Lubricant, Small Arms

LZ: Landing Zone (for helicopters)

M-16: lightweight automatic/semiautomatic machine gun, weighing 7.6 pounds; rifle used by American infantrymen

M-60: American machine gun, fed by belt of

ammunition; the gun weighs twenty-three pounds, unloaded

M-79: grenade launcher; called "thumper" or "bloop gun," due to the sound it makes when firing

MACV: Military Assistance Command Vietnam

Mad minute: a free-fire practice and test session for weapons

Magazine: holds twenty rounds (bullets) and is inserted into the M-16

Medevac: medical evacuation by helicopter; dust-off

Mermite: heavily insulated containers used to transport hot food to soldiers in the field

MOS: Military Occupational Specialty

MPC: Military Payment Certificate; currency used by American forces in Vietnam

NCO: Noncommissioned Officer

NDP: Night Defensive Position

Number one: slang for "the best"

Number ten: slang for "the worst"

NVA: North Vietnamese Army (the enemy)

OCS: Officer Candidate School

OD: olive drab

OP: Observation Post

P-38: small metal can opener used to open C-rations

PFC: Private First Class

Point: the lead man in a patrol

Post Exchange: (also, *PX*) store located on military bases where soldiers can purchase a wide variety of items; often, prices are much lower than they are in nonmilitary stores

Pot: (also, *steel pot*) slang for helmet

PRC-25: infantry radio carried by RTOs in the bush to maintain communication with the rear

Quonset hut: military structure for office and other facilities on a military base; easy to assemble and take apart; made of curved, corrugated metal

R & R: Rest and Relaxation

The rear: anyplace where noncombat support troops are located

Rock and roll: firing a weapon on full automatic

RTO: Radio-Telephone Operator

Saddle up!: order commonly given to troops at rest, indicating for them to resume marching

S & D: Search and Destroy; a mission during which troops locate, and destroy, anything the enemy might be able to use — food, weapons, shelter

Sit-rep: situation report

A skate: an easy day, mission, or task, as in "It's a skate."

Slack: the person who walks behind the point man on patrol

Smoke grenade: grenades carried by soldiers, which emit smoke in various colors; used for signaling

SOP: Standard Operating Procedure

Ti-ti: slang for "small"

TOC: Tactical Operations Center

Tracer: bullet, or round, with phosphorus on it. As the bullet is fired, the phosphorus burns, creating a visual track of the bullet's flight. Generally, every fifth round is a tracer. Particularly useful for night fighting.

Viet Cong: (also *VC, Victor Charlie*) Vietnamese communist. It refers to the National Liberation Front, which is the organization of South Vietnamese communists who were fighting against the American troops and the ARVN. The Viet Cong were under either direct, or unofficial, control of the North Vietnamese Army.

Ville: slang for village

Wake-up: last day of a soldier's tour before being sent home, as in "ten days and a wake-up"

Web gear: suspenders and belt a soldier wears to which necessary equipment can be attached, and reached more easily in an emergency (web

gear, as opposed to less essential gear, which
would be stored in a soldier's rucksack)

White phosphorus: (also *WP, Willy Pete, Willie
Peter*) refers to an incendiary artillery round,
generally used for marking a target, but also
very destructive; can also be used in grenades

WIA: (also, *Whiskey-India-Alpha*) Wounded in
Action

XO: Executive Officer

Look for ECHO COMPANY #2:
HILL 568, coming soon . . .

After only two weeks in Vietnam, the war was already worse than Michael could ever have imagined. It was going to take all of his courage and skill — and luck — to survive. In a place where a guy could be alive one second, and dead the next, it was dangerous to make friends. Close friends. But it was more dangerous *not* to have friends, and Michael was going to need every single one he could get. Because friends like Snoopy were the only thing he could really count on. The only thing that was going to keep him alive. Because Michael's war was about to get even worse.

Sergeant Hanson wanted him to start walking point.

point®

Other books you will enjoy,
about real kids like you!

THRILLERS

Gripping tales that will keep you turning from page to page—strange happenings, unsolved mysteries, and things unimaginable!

☐ MC44330-5	**The Accident** Diane Hoh	$2.95
☐ MC43115-3	**April Fools** Richie Tankersley Cusick	$2.95
☐ MC44236-8	**The Baby-sitter** R.L. Stine	$2.95
☐ MC43278-8	**Beach Party** R.L. Stine	$2.95
☐ MC43125-0	**Blind Date** R.L. Stine	$2.75
☐ MC43279-6	**The Boyfriend** R.L. Stine	$2.95
☐ MC43291-5	**Final Exam** A. Bates	$2.95
☐ MC41641-3	**The Fire** Caroline B. Cooney	$2.95
☐ MC43806-9	**The Fog** Caroline B. Cooney	$2.95
☐ MC43050-5	**Funhouse** Diane Hoh	$2.95
☐ MC43203-6	**The Lifeguard** Richie Tankersley Cusick	$2.75
☐ MC42515-3	**My Secret Admirer** Carol Ellis	$2.75
☐ MC44238-4	**Party Line** A. Bates	$2.95
☐ MC44237-6	**Prom Dress** Lael Littke	$2.95
☐ MC43014-9	**Slumber Party** Christopher Pike	$2.75
☐ MC41640-5	**The Snow** Caroline B. Cooney	$2.75
☐ MC43280-X	**The Snowman** R.L. Stine	$2.95
☐ MC43114-5	**Teacher's Pet** Richie Tankersley Cusick	$2.95
☐ MC44235-X	**Trick or Treat** Richie Tankersley Cusick	$2.95
☐ MC43139-0	**Twisted** R.L. Stine	$2.75
☐ MC44256-2	**Weekend** Christopher Pike	$2.95

Available wherever you buy books, or use this order form.